The Dr. Naomi Alexander Series

Previews of Books 1-3

S.F. Powell

Nib Karatasi Press, Upper Marlboro, MD

For permission requests, write to the publisher, addressed "Attention: Permissions Coordinator," at this address: ACT3 Enterprises, LLC–Nib Karatasi Press, PO Box 4726, Upper Marlboro, MD 20775

Online contact: visit www.sfpowell.com

Publisher's Note: This is a work of fiction. Names, characters, places, and incidents are a product of the author's imagination. Locales and public names are sometimes used for atmospheric purposes. Any resemblance to actual people, living or dead, or to businesses, companies, events, institutions, or locales is completely coincidental. The author is not a doctor. This work of fiction is for entertainment only and is not intended as a substitute for the medical advice of real physicians. The reader should regularly consult a licensed physician in matters relating to their mental/ physical health.

Like Sweet Buttermilk / S.F. Powell

Library of Congress Control Number: 2023901550

ISBNs: 978-1-7327224-0-8 / 978-1-7327224-1-5 / 978-1-7327224-2-2

Obscure Boundaries / S.F. Powell

Library of Congress Control Number: 2023901549

ISBNs: 978-1-7327224-3-9 / 978-1-7327224-4-6 / 978-1-7327224-5-3

Broken Benevolence / S.F. Powell

Library of Congress Control Number: 2023906793

ISBNs: 978-1-7327224-6-0 / 978-1-7327224-7-7 / 978-1-7327224-8-4

Like Sweet Buttermilk

Book 1

Chapter 1

Dinner for Two

For whatever reason, the "romantic" evening irritated rather than delighted. And there were several potential contributors.

Dinner was only so-so. The Cajun catfish? Dry. The rice? Overcooked.

But primarily, the skulking irritation stemmed from the awkward silences filling the fits and starts of conversation.

Society made much over a woman's intuition. But men had it, too. What they did with it? Well, now, that was the thing.

Richard "Rick" Phillips rubbed his eyes with the thumb and index finger of his left hand, trying to ease the subtle but persistent hammer taps behind his right eye. He sat across from his wife, Vivian, staring past her into the night movements of downtown Washington, DC.

He shifted his gaze to her. "So, a family vacation is out?"

"I'm saying we may have to postpone it." She rolled her eyes with an annoyed sigh. "You always go to extremes, Rick. Did you hear me say a family vacation was out? No, you didn't." She studied her plate, forking around the food left uneaten.

And there it was again: that (irritating) awkward silence—the unwelcomed third party at this dinner for two.

Men possessed a certain level of intuition, too.

Rick reached for his right ear. The scar there always provided an odd comfort. He fingered it while staring at his wife, allowing the skulking irritation to *intuit* him...because something was off.

Her new haircut was more flattering than he expected. He liked her below-shoulder-length hair, so when she hinted at getting it cut, he stopped short of going caveman on her and "forbidding" such a move.

Styled in a bob, Viv's hair framed her face softly despite its blunt cut as the restaurant lighting kissed the natural auburn highlights in her chestnut hair. He loved her hair: soft, rich in color, and thick. Pushing a hand deep into her hair while kissing or getting busy with her always added an arousing bonus.

Rick stopped his wife's hand from pushing her fork around, wanting her to look at him.

He didn't understand why the evening floundered. Couldn't understand why a romantic occasion seemed forced and staged, as if going through the motions for some unseen director. "Look at me, Viv." He used a tone warm and encouraging.

She lifted those eyes to him. Viv's eyes were gorgeous: wide and round like a child's but sultry—the irises rare: dark as the blackest coal (and not the darkest brown anything).

God, he loved her.

"Rick, I don't want—"

"I know. You don't want to get into a 'thing.' But we're not go'n get into anything because you're the one upset, not me." He paused, mentally assessing the last few days. "And, as far as I know, I have done nothing. But I know you, Viv: something's wrong."

She exhaled heavily, glancing around DeTante's. "I'm just tired. I told you I didn't want to eat here for our night out." Her eyes darted about almost feverishly.

Rick surveyed the restaurant, too, trying to find what she was looking for. He took another bite of dry fish. "That you did. But we've eaten at several places since we were here last. DeTante's is *our* place." He raised an eyebrow. "Why so anti-DeTante's lately?" This was the most they'd said all evening.

Their server, Jorge, approached. "Everything okay?"

"We're good. Can I get an Elijah Craig Twenty-three, neat?" Rick turned to his wife. "Viv?" Her mind seemed elsewhere.

Oh yeah, something was up.

"Oh. An espresso. Thanks, Jorge." She smiled, sending Jorge away.

Viv had a beautiful smile: warm and soft, friendly yet flirty in certain clandestine moments. But she also possessed this confident, dazzling smile that made his heart skip a beat. He hadn't seen *that* smile of hers for some time.

He called it her "best-present" smile: a smile coming when one opens that "best present, ever." The smile wasn't too big, showing too many teeth, but it was generous and sincere, winning his heart every time.

Not this time, though. This time, her smile appeared weak and somewhat sad, and Rick's concern edged into more irritation. He hated solving problems indirectly.

"Vivian." His light tone camouflaged his annoyance.

"Yes?" Viv's tone mimicked his.

"Look, let's get to it. It's obvious something's bothering you, but usually, you're right out with it. So, tell me."

Okay, the last sentence sounded more like a command than gentle prodding, but this was getting old, and none of this hemming-and-hawing helped his headache.

Another sigh from her, this one infused with an uptight weariness. "Okay, Rick, look. You know how much I love y—"

"What's up, Phillipses?! Long time no see." As he approached their table, Jonathan Rast, DeTante's owner, imparted elation with eyes wide and welcoming.

Rick shook his hand. "Hey, man. Yeah, it's been a while. How's it going?" He started rising, but Jonathan gestured for him to stay seated.

"Pretty good. Can't complain." Jonathan shook Viv's hand as Jorge returned with their drinks.

"Anything for you, Mister Rast?"

"I'm good, Jorge. Thanks."

Viv looked up at Jonathan as Jorge retreated, her eyes filled with caring worry. "How's your mom, Jonathan?"

Rick could tell she appreciated the interruption. He thought about her prefacing whatever she was going to say with a reiteration of her love. Now honestly, what good could follow that?

"Guess I spoke too soon. The Alzheimer's is taking its toll; we don't expect her to be with us much longer." Jonathan shook his head as if clearing any sadness. "But, I'm not here for the gloom and doom. Just passing through. It's been a minute since seeing you two in here together, so I came over. All's well?"

Rick read genuine concern on his face, but Jonathan gazed at Viv with the question, directing his concern more toward her. And "in here *together*" was an interesting choice of words. That phrasing didn't sit well, triggering a coil of unhappiness inside him, and Rick wondered what his limits were concerning Viv. He was an even-tempered dude, but that coil of despair gave him pause—imparted a clue to how far his limits reached (or *didn't* reach) regarding his wife.

He let it go. "All's well." Rick glanced at Viv. "Nuthin' major going on."

Jonathan pulled a chair from a neighboring table and sat.

Rick released a quiet breath of relief; the neck strain from looking up at him didn't help his headache.

Jonathan stretched out, resting his hands atop his head. He'd decided to visit awhile.

Rick didn't mind. He was in no hurry to hear whatever was about to follow Viv's opening line, anyway.

They settled into general conversation, but Rick's attention wavered. Viv's mood changed for the better—and now something about that bothered him, too. But again, he didn't focus on it. Between the so-so meal and the lack of conversation and the headache and the whatever else, his irritation sprouted, reaching for everything—perhaps unfairly.

Perhaps.

Watching her, though, he recalled how they found DeTante's.

They found DeTante's by chance—a missed subway stop during a rendezvous for their twelfth wedding anniversary. He fondly remembered their night stroll downtown and Viv wanting to detour into the nook of a deserted photography studio for a quickie. How (his erection straining as she caressed and squeezed all over it) he woefully rejected her. He couldn't ignore being in public; taking things further wasn't an option. Viv couldn't have cared less. If things were tasteful, she wanted sex wherever.

Turned out, the "photography studio" was DeTante's: an upscale three-tiered restaurant with southern cuisine and soul food, a photography-themed decor, and the ever-present sound of flutes playing overhead. They met Jonathan that first night when he stopped by their table to greet new patrons. Rick remembered being uncomfortable and territorial over Viv that night.

Over the years, they returned to DeTante's at least monthly. The atmosphere and southern cuisine rarely failed them. In that respect, DeTante's became their place.

Until tonight, apparently.

Rick came in and out of this reverie while contributing to the light-fare conversation. He enjoyed Jonathan's table visits (having grown less territorial over Viv).

He particularly noticed Viv's improved mood; it was brighter (*Okay, Rick, look. You know how much I love you...*), but she still didn't smile much (so something lingered).

"Oh, you'll be surprised next time you're here." Jonathan's words brought Rick back to the discussion at hand.

Viv's eyes widened with recognition. "When will they be up?"

"I expect to add to the series during downtime this weekend, so, sometime next week." Jonathan stood and stretched.

"Then we'll be back next week with Alna. Right, Rick?"

Mentioning Alna clued Rick in. About a year ago, Viv took up photography again. Even Alna caught the photographer's bug. Some Saturdays, Viv and Alna would have a girls' day out, shooting pictures instead of shopping. Rick had an appreciative eye for Viv's shots, and Alna's images showed promise, too.

Shortly after New Year's, he suggested submitting the photos to Jonathan for display at DeTante's, as many of her images aligned with the restaurant's theme. It was March now; he'd heard nothing more about it. He grinned, thinking about his daughter's reaction to the news; she'll be overjoyed.

Rick gave a single head nod. "Damn skippy."

The intimation behind Viv being in contact with Jonathan without him crossed his mind, but disappeared into thoughts of a family outing.

He valued family time. Viv would say he "obsessed" over it, but he welcomed additional opportunities for the three to be together. Viv appreciated family time but considered time alone equally necessary.

"Next week, then." Jonathan plucked his leather bag and jacket from the neighboring table. After giving Rick a power handshake, he turned to Viv. "I'll also have the shots we didn't use, okay?" He kissed her cheek.

Now, for years, Jonathan gave him the power handshake and Viv the customary kiss on the cheek. Rick never had a problem with it. Didn't have a problem now. Jonathan's kiss was cool: a brush of his lips, barely touching Viv.

The kiss was fine.

Viv's reaction was not.

She smiled. Given she hadn't smiled much all evening, Rick welcomed it. But the smile grew into her best-present smile; the one that warmed him inside.

Viv smiled that smile, directed at Jonathan, not at him—and the pain in his head sharpened from clenching his teeth.

"Okay, next week then," she confirmed, that smile fading as quickly as it had come. But it was too late.

Rick turned to Jonathan. "A'ight, bruh. Catch you later. Our prayers are with your family, man."

Jonathan nodded his thanks, signaled Jorge to return, and was gone.

Jorge arrived, inquiring about dessert.

Rick had a taste for DeTante's pecan pie. His taste for it was gone now. He ordered it anyway.

Jorge turned to Viv.

"I was gonna pass, but since Rick ordered something, I guess I'll have a scoop of vanilla to go with his pie." She winked at Rick.

"I could order the pie à la mode and bring two spoons, ma'am."

"No thanks, Jorge. We'll do the mixing ourselves. Right, baby?"

"Beg pardon?" Her mood reflected a total 180-degree turn. "Uh, sure."

Excitement about the photos probably carried over from Jonathan's visit. But this sudden bold flirting confused him. Forty-five minutes ago, he could guarantee sex was a no-go.

He knew Viv; she wanted sex. But where was this coming from?

An awkward silence ensued while they awaited dessert, but it lingered with a distinct air. Earlier, the silences stemmed from tension between two people trying to avoid some unpleasantness (although he had no idea what the unpleasantness was). This silence pulsed with sexual tension, putting him on edge. The smile Viv gave Jonathan upset him, but regardless, her suggestive words and flirtatious looks turned him on. As did her walking into a room.

Viv reached for his hand and caressed it. She often said she loved his hands. When her desire to make love burgeoned, she sometimes let him know by taking his hand and stroking it seductively as she did now.

The muscles in his groin stirred, but he pulled his hand away, pretending a need to scratch his shoulder.

Jorge served their desserts.

As he headed away, Viv dug in.

Rick couldn't take it anymore. "So, what's up?"

She frowned, murmuring, "Huh?" around a spoonful of vanilla.

"I could barely get two sentences out of you earlier, let alone interest you in any *after-dinner activity*. Now you're acting more like you, so I don't get it." He leaned toward her, getting sexy whiffs of her body oil. She wore the orchids-and-cinnamon one tonight: one of his favorites on her. "Before Jonathan came, you were trying to tell me something. What was it?" He gazed around the restaurant before sitting back. "You started saying something about knowing how much you love me, but you didn't get to finish."

Viv pointed her spoon at his plate. "You gonna eat your pie?" She ate another spoonful of ice cream.

The pie was warm: Jorge's special touch (warranting a boost in his tip). "Yes, I am. What were you go'n say?"

"I don't know. Guess I wanted to say, you know I love you and these nights out, but tonight I wasn't up for it. I told you I was tired, but sometimes good news can bring you around." She reached over, scooping a spoonful of his pie. "And you must admit: Jonathan was a bearer of good news, telling us our photos would be on display. So, I'm excited about next week, and I feel bad about how I acted toward you earlier. See? No big deal. Now eat your pie so we can go." She ate her spoonful of pecan pie à la mode, eyeing him with meaning.

Rick gazed back calmly. He didn't believe her.

The part about being excited over the pictures sounded plausible. But the rest of it? No.

There were no telltale signs she was lying: no eye twitching, word stuttering, or eye contact avoidance. Rick didn't have any historical basis for not believing her, either—but he didn't. Basic math. But he'd wait it out.

They finished dessert in comfortable silence.

Rick retrieved his wallet.

"I got it this time."

"That'll work. I got the tip, though."

She fixed him with an alluring gaze. "So, you ready?" She fancied using that double entendre sometimes.

And, despite all the irritation and concern and suspicion, her effect on him, as always, was instant. "...Damn skippy." He winked at her, then stood to get her coat, purposely giving her a view of his semi.

The gaze in those sable irises lingered below his waist before meeting his eyes, and the edges of her lips turned upward with sultry gaiety. "Then let's go."

Viv took his hand as they strolled to the car.

After fifteen years of marriage, Rick understood things changed—the honeymoon didn't last forever. Routine set in. Yet nights like tonight (minus the tense first hour or two) more than outnumbered any down-turns, so overall, he and Viv were doing well, their relationship solid.

Chuckling, he opened the passenger door for her. Viv's blush-colored dress was perfect for the evening and fit her shapely form to full effect. The cinnamon in her body oil teased, encouraging his thoughts toward some nice, pulsing, after-dinner activity.

"What's so funny?"

"Thinking about our college days."

She brushed his hand with hers before getting in. "Yeah, and...?"

"How you didn't want to be bothered at first."

Viv quirked her lips. "Not with those jokes you kept telling."

Rick scoffed, closed her door, and settled in the driver's seat. "Give me a break; I was nervous, trying to make an impression," he offered, playfully defensive. "It got you talking to me." He turned the ignition.

"Rick, please. Those jokes were so corny." She giggled.

"Yeah, but you finally agreed to go out—even after learning I was two years younger." He pulled into traffic.

"Well, you were corny, but cute. Your appreciation for music from the seventies put you over, though." She touched his cheek. "And I had a problem with the age difference, attending different schools. Louise convinced me to date you, anyway."

"'Age difference'? You make two years sound like twenty."

"Oh, when you're a senior dating a sophomore, two years can seem like twenty."

"And here we are: eighteen years later. Two still feeling like twenty?"

Viv lowered her hand and turned to her window. "No."

"Hey, what's wrong?"

She shook her head in reply.

This recent moodiness was one of the post-honeymoon changes. He couldn't pinpoint when her moodiness started; he just wanted it to end. They had little problem communicating over matters, good or bad. They weren't Cliff and Clair Huxtable. There'd been a mistake on his part (or three, if counting), but they were exceptional together.

He waited at a stoplight. Traffic was light for late evening. He lowered the windows a crack, then placed a hand on Viv's thigh.

She rested her hand on his, still peering through her window.

Rick watched the night, waiting for the light to change.

He smiled, thinking about the day they met, remembering watching her from several rows behind during an economics lecture on campus; how time stopped, and his heart fluttered with the potent wonderment cloaking him as she looked over her shoulder to check the clock...

They were married in a small, intimate ceremony soon after he graduated from George Mason. His brother, David, was his best man. He remembered Dave being more nervous than he was. Not wanting to think about David, Rick shifted his thoughts to Alna.

They'd been married five years when they were finally blessed with Alna. Viv wanted a boy, and Rick, so pleased at the prospect of being a daddy, didn't care what sex the baby was, fully adopting the whole as-long-as-it's-healthy perspective. Alna was a joy: sweet, affectionate—with enough tomboy in her for Viv to appreciate. And they did have their baby boy, but...

Off and on (despite losing two babies), they entertained having another sibling for Alna. But lately (as during the early part of their date), Viv avoided discussing subjects relating to their family.

The brisk night air helped ease his headache ("sleeping weather," his mother called it). Mistakes and moodiness aside, they weren't a statistic—and wouldn't be. His family meant everything to him. Even with the mistakes he'd made, his family meant absolutely everything. He'd do whatever it took to keep it together.

Family was important.

As he turned into their driveway on Bard o' Avon Court, an image of Viv smiling at Jonathan popped into his head. He pondered the smile (that coil of unhappiness presenting again), but Viv's hand moved, stroking him gently.

Once parked in their garage, Rick leaned over and kissed his wife, and all was right again as her tongue danced with his.

But something in her kiss told him,...not as right as it used to be.

Chapter 2

Ain't Love Grand?

Mixed emotions. Viv tried concentrating on responding to Rick's kiss. She loved kissing him (his kiss was like no other's), but her emotions interfered with giving in as she wanted.

He'd asked if two years felt like twenty.

In terms of their age difference? No. But the question prompted thoughts of other aspects of their life together recently, so she hesitated before answering.

There were reasons things faltered as of late, but she was caught between Rick's devotion to family and not wanting to hurt him versus wanting a break from things. And breaking from Rick meant hurting them both, so...

Ambivalence aside, his kiss got to her. Viv brought her husband closer, getting more of his sweet tongue. Kisses didn't lie; his kiss was all that, every time. Bottom line: she wanted him.

She owned a healthy sexual appetite, having no problem letting Rick know what she wanted. There were instances of being less in the mood (naturally), but overall, she thoroughly enjoyed sex and wanted it often.

This didn't involve any sexual peak associated with her age, either. She enjoyed sex in her 20s and 30s. And as she approached 40, if healthy, her senior years would be no different.

"Let's see if Nora got Al off to bed." She played with Rick's necktie, gazing into his eyes. His irises were captivating; this warm golden-auburn, lightened with red and dark-gold tones: extra gorgeous when sunlight hit them. Looking into Rick's eyes was like gazing into a cozy fire. She tapped the cleft in his chin. "If not, I'll get little Miss

Missy tucked in, then meet you in the sunroom." She opened her car door instead of waiting for Rick to open it.

"So, the sunroom tonight. Should I open the windows?" His inquiry was soft and suggestive, giving her pleasant tingles. He didn't balk at the idea this time; it surprised her.

"That would be best." Viv exited the car, feeling his eyes on her as she walked toward the door leading into their laundry room.

Rick closed his door. "You know Alna isn't asleep. Nora adores her, so Al gets to do pretty much as she pleases. Basic math. Now, *Tracie's* a different story."

She turned back. "Please. Tracie adores her, too, but Al doesn't get away with too much because Tracie's older and can resist many of Alna's wiles. Now come on, so I can get this girl to bed. I know she's up."

He raised an eyebrow; an expression that consistently generated something nice-and-swirly in her. "What's your hurry?"

Viv smiled at the incredibly handsome man and entered the house.

It was ten forty-seven p.m. Low sound emitted from the television in their sunken family room; otherwise, the house was quiet. Nora was asleep on the sofa, her schoolbooks stacked on the floor. The faint, distinct stench of burned food lingered, and the unusual quiet only emphasized it.

Rick entered, standing behind her. "Okay, this is different. Now, if Al's asleep, I'll know we're in the twilight zone." He placed a hand on her waist. "You goin' up?"

"Yeah." She wrinkled her nose. "I wonder what culinary masterpiece burned in my kitchen."

"Who knows? I'll get Nora." He kissed her temple.

Viv headed across the kitchen into the hallway. As she ascended the stairs, she saw light illuminating from the bottom clearance of the closed door of the hall bath.

A prickle of unease nipped her nape; the tranquility spooked her.

When she and Rick came home from a night out, if Nora was the sitter, Alna greeted them with hugs and tales of the evening. Viv almost expected it. Tonight, however, equated more with occasions Tracie babysat for them. Light came from Alna's bedroom to the right. The remaining three bedrooms were dark.

She knocked on the bathroom door. "Al?"

"Hi, Mommy." Alna sounded small, tired. "You can come in." The definitive whoosh of the toilet flushing followed.

Viv opened the door. "What's wrong, sweetie?" She watched her daughter pat water on her cheeks and chin.

"I didn't want regular dinner, so Nora said I could fix something else, as long as I was sure I was gonna eat it." Alna's voice and words fluctuated within the towel as she dried her face. "So, I fixed somethin' I knew I would ea—"

"Alna, you did not have a PB-and-J with sardines on the side again, did you?" Viv held back a gag thinking about it. *Rick and his concoctions.*

"Uh-huh, but Nora said I couldn't have the whole can, so I only had two fishes." Alna held up two fingers, looking cute in her sports-gear pajamas. Nora put one large french braid down the middle of Al's head and added gold barrettes to each side.

"*Fish*, in this case, Alna, not 'fishes.'"

"Oil or mustard sauce?" Rick stepped up behind them.

Alna grinned, beaming at her father. "Mustard."

Viv turned to him.

"That's my girl." He winked at Alna.

Viv loved Rick's bond with their daughter. It rooted her ambivalent feelings. She turned back to Alna. "So now your stomach's upset. Is it number two? Number three?" She checked Alna's forehead and neck for signs of temperature.

"Number three. But, Mommy, I was fine with my dinner. Smelling the burned cheese sauce made me sick." She lowered her eyes, studying her wriggling toes.

"...Been messing with the microwave, Alna?" Rick's mellow tone lost its playfulness.

Al shook her head.

Viv put a hand on Rick's arm; she had this one. "What happened, honey?" Alna usually owned up to her mistakes.

"Nothing. Nora had nachos, but she burned the cheese sauce by accident." Al's eyes were wide.

Viv's heart tugged, but she kept a straight face, wondering if children were born knowing how to use that skill. "Okay, sweetie."

Alna focused on her father, reading his expression.

Viv did the same.

Rick didn't appear upset. He stood, hands in his pockets. His fine ass looked good, too. Good enough to eat...

He picked up her vibe. Without another word, he kissed Alna's forehead and palmed her head affectionately. As he turned to leave the bathroom, he air-kissed Viv and winked.

Warm stirrings trembled low in Viv's belly. Ready for some after-dinner activity, she turned back to Alna. "Feeling better?"

"Guess so. Daddy was right about putting cold water on your face when you feel pukey."

"Yeah, your daddy has lots of good ideas rolling around in his brain. Come on; time for bed." Viv turned out the light and left the bathroom for Alna's room—Al right on her heels.

"Did you and Daddy have fun?"

"We just went to dinner, sweetie, not a wild safari or anything." Viv patted Alna's bed. "Come on; hop up."

Alna climbed in, snuggling down low. "Did you go where Mister Rast works?" A simple question, but it bothered Viv.

"We did." She postponed sharing Jonathan's good news.

"Daddy likes that place. I kinda do, too; you guys don't let me go enough." Alna wore a slight pout. The expression made Viv think of her mother, whom she missed dearly.

"Well, that's our special place to be together, but we've taken you plenty of times. Besides, we regularly trek to Zibby's Fun Palace, and you have a ball. Shouldn't Mommy and Daddy go someplace for grownups, with foods besides pizza and no noisy games?"

"I guess. So, did you have fun?"

"What is it with you and this 'fun'? It was dinner, sweetie."

"But you went to a favorite place. Doesn't that make it fun?" Alna was genuine in her wanting to know.

"Honey, grownups and children have different ways of viewing things as fun. But, yeah, we had a good time. How's that?" Viv wasn't sure where her daughter was going with this *fun* angle, but she hoped her answer quelled further pursuit.

"You mean, when I grow up, things won't be fun anymore?" Her upper lip curled with curious unhappiness.

So much for quelling further pursuit. "They'll be fun, honey, just *different* fun."

Alna folded her arms over her chest, her pout serious. "Then I don't wanna grow up. I like fun the way it is now. Why does grownup fun have to be different? When Nora talks to her boyfriend on the phone, she sounds like she's having fun, and she's an almost-grownup." Eyes widening with interest, she rose from under the covers. "Is love fun? When does the different fun start?"

Viv halted Al from climbing out altogether. "Whoa there, Miss Missy; slow down." She resumed tucking her in. "I don't know why or even *if* grownup fun should be different; it just is. And there is no set time for when it changes. One day you just find that it has. And, yes, love is fun, or at least it should be." Viv could not believe she was having this discussion with her nine-year-old.

"Fun should be fun no matter how old you are," Alna concluded. "You love Daddy, right?"

"Of course. Very much." She warmed with the declaration.

"And you said love was fun. So, is love-fun different, too?"

Thinking about Rick's twilight zone comment, Viv's lips slanted into a wry smile.

Who let this child in here?

"Sweetie, it's time for bed. Mommy doesn't have any suitable answers for you now. But I'll think about it and try to explain it better later. Okay?" Viv leaned close with a pucker.

Alna kissed her goodnight.

Viv turned out the light on Al's nightstand. "Candy castles and ice cream rivers." It was her mother's version of "sweet dreams," whispered whenever she put Viv and her sister, Patrice, to bed.

A lump rose in her throat. She didn't know why thoughts of her mother kept surfacing.

"G'night, Mommy." The distinct rustle of covers accompanied Alna's getting more comfortable.

Viv paused in the doorway. "Sure, your tummy's better?"

"Uh-huh." Alna already sounded sleepy.

Viv closed the door.

They were home all of fifteen minutes, but it seemed much longer. Viv anticipated meeting Rick downstairs, but wanted to freshen first. She decided against lingerie, opting for her silk robe—and nothing else.

Viv walked through the double-door entrance to their bedroom, lifting her dress over her head and tossing it onto the cedar chest at the foot of their king-sized bed.

I'm going to miss this room.

She froze, wondering where the thought came from. She hadn't decided anything.

Is love fun?

She lounged across the bed with a sigh, thinking about Alna's question. She told Alna that, at the very least, love should be fun. And Viv believed that to be true. Her marriage, however, declined in the fun department ever (since Jonathan) since Rick's last incident years ago. But Viv didn't care as much anymore now that she had (Jonathan) a different perspective on things.

Given her conversation with Alna, Viv questioned her marriage-happiness quotient. She stared at the African-print rug centering their bedroom, reflecting on the one time she and Rick made ardent love on it. The image of their brown bodies mingling with the backdrop of the rug's tribal pattern remained an erotic memory. She often wanted to make love on the rug, but overall, Rick was a bed man. For reasons unknown to her, he preferred sex in their bed. After seventeen years of intimacy with him, she still didn't know what that was about.

There were some exceptions, however. The sunroom tonight would be one; the one time on the rug; and another time last Christmas when she insisted on making love in the sunroom with a view of the Christmas lights twinkling in the family room. She told Rick she wanted the windows opened if they ever did it in the sunroom in a warmer month. She was stunned Rick remembered (or even entertained getting busy in the sunroom again).

Viv turned over. Hands behind her head, she gazed at the ceiling fan. There were other occasions (like a time or two on their bedroom balcony), but overall, her husband preferred a bed for intimacy. She grunted with phantom sensation from past off-the-chain indulgences with him. In all honesty, location didn't matter. Wherever they did it, the shit was good.

However, Rick's reluctance to make love outside their bedroom didn't strike the heart of her discontent. It was a factor of the bigger problem.

She was growing, changing (bored). And at 39, she was tired of trying to get Rick to revisit his wild side. His devotion to their family was terrific (sometimes weird), but at what cost?

Viv sat up. She didn't want to think right now, but she decided on something: she needed time and a break to consider the future of her marriage. She'd tell Rick what was going on with her soon (tomorrow?), but not tonight. Rick was downstairs, waiting. Regardless of her feelings about separating, their sex was amazing; she wanted her husband.

She swallowed a laugh at the irony of contemplating leaving her now considerably less adventurous husband on a night he seemed most spontaneous, like his old self.

Is love fun?

Well, love hadn't been *much* fun for some time. But it would be shortly. Viv unhooked her bra and entered their en suite to get ready.

She came downstairs, expecting to find Rick asleep in the family room, the television glowing. She found darkness instead. The only sound was the night, heard through the open sunroom windows as a breeze rustled the budding trees.

Rick stood off to the side of their sunroom, looking out the window. Except for shoes, he was dressed—so that she could undress him. Removing his clothing (especially loosening his necktie and opening his pants) spurred her excitement.

He held a glass of something in his left hand by his side. Probably iced tea: his preferred beverage.

Even in silhouette, Viv appreciated her husband's good looks. Rick was slim but muscular: just under six feet three and circling 165 pounds. A fifth-degree black belt in karate, his martial-arts training showed. He didn't have broad shoulders (like Jonathan). Nevertheless, he possessed that masculine V.

A breeze rustled again, carrying Rick's cologne to her: he wore John Varvatos' Artisan Black.

His fragrance, the sounds of the night, enticed her. Her nipples hardened from the cool air, brushing her silk robe against them. She went to Rick, encircling him from behind. Peering around him, she followed his gaze, taking in the view.

Their house backed to deep woods bordering Route 301 on the other side of the trees. Intermittent traffic echoed in the distance. The clear night rendered moonlight shining through the skylights, near perfection in its contribution to the evening. Essentially, it was dark, the yard below black. Plants adorned the windows, obscuring any view of them: Viv didn't worry about being seen.

She hugged Rick tighter. He released a deep sigh but didn't move: this interlude belonged to her. Viv rested her forehead on his upper back (she loved his strong back), breathing in all the goodness of his JV Artisan Black. "I love you, Rick."

"I know. I love you." Tension filled his reply. "Want music?"

"No..." She guided him to face her. Holding his face in her hands, she kissed him. Their tongues blended tenderly, his mouth tasting of iced tea (sweet with a hint of lemon).

Rick still held his glass. Viv broke their kiss and collected it, placing it on the table beside them, then took his hand, leading him to the roomier side of their sunroom. She held Rick's gaze for a beat before pressing against his body and getting more of his iced-tea tongue.

He rested his fingertips at her waist—an innocent but classic move of his. All these years, he still knew nothing of its effect on her. The light pressure of his touch radiated both masculine power and a gentleness conveying his sexual prowess.

Mouth locked with Rick's, Viv backed him to the wall. She intensified the aggression of her kiss until he raised his hands in casual surrender. Nibbling Rick's soft lips (and getting a thrill from the brush of hair above them), she gradually released the Diagonal knot in his tie and unbuttoned his shirt.

Having him against the wall made her want to abandon preliminaries and take what she wanted.

She also wanted to cradle her husband's head to her breast and let him suckle himself to sleep (as she had many times before).

Viv lowered Rick's arms, removing his shirt by drawing her hands over his shoulders. She broke from his mouth just long enough for him to remove his A-shirt, then kissed his neck and chest, trailing hands down his rocklike torso.

Rick cleared his throat, a sound gravelly, rolling. Over the years, she'd learned his varied throat-clearings. They ranged from one denoting blushing and uncomfortable to another expressing contemplative inquiry, to one signaling concern or annoyance, to this one—conveying utter arousal.

She held his gaze as she opened his belt, giving him a wink. This interlude belonged to her.

He echoed a hushed chuckle and tilted his head back, wearing this crooked grin both knowing and sexy.

Viv lowered to his crotch. Clutching his rear, she kissed her husband's powerful erection through his pants (sometimes using her teeth) before unzipping and freeing him. The semi-dark did nothing to obscure how naturally blessed her husband was.

She encircled him with a hand and stroked all those inches lightly, making him moan.

He pushed fingers through her hair, caressing her scalp while she pursued oral exploration. Viv mouthed everything without haste, tasting lotion and mountain-fresh soap tinged with his oils.

Rick pulled back as she got into it, though. If she wanted something different, he couldn't let that continue.

Because she did want something different, Viv stood. Trailing a finger over his left biceps, she gazed at the delightful reveal while he finished undressing, removing his pants and boxers.

Impatient now, she moved close and gripped his hardness again, stroking his length as he opened her robe. His breathing was low and shuddery, which only excited her more; the *sounds* of sex (especially male arousal) always did something to her.

Viv ran her eyes over his diced body: cinnamon-brown muscles rippled everywhere, and something definitively male jutted toward her, hot and hard in her hand. Her body pulsing, she licked her lips in anticipation. Rick was... Oh, yeah.

Power and aggression coursed through her, fusing with anger and regret at realizing that even with this hotness between them, a part of her wanted to separate.

Viv observed her husband, loving him beyond measure—and then loving him not so much.

Rick's scents enticed her: his soap, his cologne, the rainforest smell of his hair. Air from the opened windows tickled her flesh.

The cool breeze on her perspiring skin didn't suppress the heat within. So, she took things further: she slapped him.

His head rocked because the slap was unexpected, but Rick returned her gaze. Seconds passed. Clouds shifted over the moon, making it harder to read his eyes.

Viv knew better, but she waited, anticipating defending herself if necessary...but also waiting to continue their lovemaking.

Rick grasped her throat. He pulled her to him, slamming his mouth against hers and driving his tongue into the deep corners of her mouth, sending her arousal higher. He didn't choke her but held her to him firmly, his erection jabbing her abdomen. His right hand moved over her breasts, kneading them and tweaking each nipple with stimulating care before moving his hand elsewhere, anywhere on her. His touch continuously reaffirmed his expertise with her body.

He spun her around and forced her over the arm of the settee, yanking her robe above her rear. Cool night air chilled the moisture of her wet and ready parts. His hand slid forward, holding the back of her neck.

Viv tried rising in "protest," her blood running warm and tingly with the scenario.

Rick held her down, using his legs to spread her wider. He paused and then teased the tip of his hardness against his possibilities, making pointed use of her wetness.

Such vulnerability made her climax. She moaned into the settee cushions with the pleasure moving through her. *This man...*

Taking the path of least resistance, Rick uttered a soft, masculine moan of her name, which said everything. He entered her gently but held her down, thrusting forcefully but with sensual rhythm.

Ignoring the faint pressure inside, Viv moved with him. Her husband (God bless him) held back his climax, allowing her to have another. She wanted one with him. She concentrated her energies, working her muscles on him with a womanly precision delivering two-fold separate but equal pleasure.

"Shit, girl..." Rick moaned low and slowed his thrusts to savor the sensation; he often did before exploding inside her. Quivering heat exuded from her thighs, rising to circle her sweet center as the minutes of goodness stretched. Her second release arrived with the flowing warmth of Rick's.

She couldn't have timed it better.

The urge to cry surfaced.

Viv shut that down.

"You okay, Viv?"

"...Yes."

They remained connected, Rick lightly caressing her hips and rear. She didn't like him pulling out immediately; it brought on a sense of loss. He guided her toward him for a kiss, their tongues moving with languid satisfaction as he massaged a breast. She liked this part, too.

When his erection subsided, he pecked her lips and stepped back, but the feeling of loss affected her, anyway; it always did.

Viv faced him. She couldn't see his eyes very well, but his pearly whites beamed her way. She smiled back. Arms around his neck, she reclaimed his mouth, sending a hand to caress his hair's dry but crinkly soft coils.

Their tongue twirl lasted quiet seconds before Rick pulled back with a grin. He picked up his clothing.

Viv took his hand, and they headed upstairs in silence.

After showering, Viv sprawled across their bed, preferring to lounge and air-dry. The cool air closed her pores, but that was okay; she didn't feel like moisturizing.

Rick toweled off in the bathroom doorway.

They had yet to speak. Viv enjoyed the unusual silence between them, accented only by the whir of the ceiling fan.

She propped on an elbow, watching her husband prepare for bed. Rick usually shaved at night to save time in the mornings, making for three o'clock rather than five o'clock shadow. He prepared to shave but stopped, apparently changing his mind. Viv hoped he'd also abandon wearing pajamas, but Rick reached in his drawer, pulling out a T-shirt and lounge pants: her luck had run out.

Viv sat up. What difference did it make?

If you're separating from him, it shouldn't matter if he was nude or wearing four layers of thermals.

But it wasn't that simple.

Chill bumps prickled her arms. She needed to moisturize, but she didn't want to move. Her body was pleasantly spent, but her mind raced (*Is love fun?*). Viv dragged herself into their bathroom, deciding to lotion with a lavender scent: maybe it'll bring on the sleepiness eluding her.

When she reentered their bedroom, Rick's sound breathing greeted her: sleep hadn't eluded him.

She retrieved a nighttime-bra and satin nightshirt from her dresser and put them on (not bothering with panties), then went to her husband and watched him sleep. He wasn't a snorer; his breathing was deep and even. "Come what may, Rick, I love you."

After donning her headwrap, Viv entered their sitting room and reclined on the loveseat to think, drawing the afghan blanket around her.

More thinking, however, didn't last long: she fell asleep.

Somewhere in her dreams were photographs of children at play.

"...Today?" Rick's voice.

"Huh?" Someone was shaking her foot.

"I said: think you'd like to rise and join the rest of the world today?"

"Huhn?" Viv sat up, grimacing from the pain jabbing her neck.

"I can't believe you slept in here all night. Gotta crick?"

"Yeah, I guess. Time izzit?"

"Quarter till eleven. Alna's already been in here wanting to wake you. We're supposed to be taking her to get new fish. Remember?" He sounded mildly excited.

Viv loved his voice. Rick spoke with a mellow baritone that translated beautifully when he sang, something Viv wished he did more often (his singing turned her on). Rick also spoke Italian, something else he didn't do much (but turned her on whenever he did). A faint southern cadence often flitted through his speech, influenced by his Virginia upbringing and having parents from Georgia and Alabama. The man sounded sexy as hell over the phone.

She rubbed her neck. "How could I forget? She's been bugging us about it for a week." Viv shook off the last vestiges of sleep. She'd dreamed of three women, creepily void of eyes and noses but still somehow leering with menacing smiles, screaming, "Ain't love grand?" as she bolted from a dark room. There was meaning in the dream, but Viv shook that off, too.

"And we've been putting her off for three. I'm starting breakfast. Want eggs?" Rick had already showered, shaved (unfortunately), and wore black sweats. With his physique, he looked good. But most times, she didn't care much for sweatpants on Rick because he usually wore them baggy (preventing good view of his tight butt). However, Viv indulged in several good views of him when he wore his more form-fitting joggers.

"Sure."

He headed away.

"Rick?"

He turned back to her, his eyes curious but somehow knowing (he was a reasonably intuitive dude).

"We need to talk, okay?"

He cleared his throat (concerned), issued his curt nod, and continued out the door.

Viv stood and stretched, turning her head to work out the stiffness.

They needed to talk, but she had no clue what she was going to say to him. Rick wouldn't easily accept anything she said, given his love for her and Alna. Remnant images of those "women" from that dream, however, settled it.

She may not be leaving Rick for good, but she needed a trial separation (at least).

Instead of showering, she figured she'd hit the high and low spots and be done. Viv snatched underwear from one drawer, pulled a T-shirt and jeans from another, and headed for the bathroom.

Viv showered anyway. She used the time to ruminate the few (impossible) ways she could tell her husband she was leaving him.

Chapter 3

Breaking News

V iv came out of the shower, starving. Her almond-scented lotion didn't help matters. Typically, she preferred a light breakfast, but she was glad it was Rick's Saturday to cook. He served up big country breakfasts—as opposed to her just-this-side-of-continental alternative. The aromas of scrapple cooking and potatoes frying conjured a sense of home, and unease settled in her belly.

Rick wouldn't cook the eggs until everyone was downstairs. Muffled sounds of conversation drifted up from the kitchen. Alna and Rick were waiting for her.

She wasn't ready.

Sitting at her vanity, Viv brushed her hair into a ponytail. She missed being able to pull it back into a longer one, but the shorter ponytail, which swept upward rather than back, made for an even fresher, carefree style. And with the summer months approaching, the carefree interested her very much. When she was 16, her father had been steadfast against cutting her hair. She remembered Rick being opposed to the idea months ago.

Rick opened their drapes to allow extra light in, but Viv wanted fresh air to circulate, too; she opened a few windows.

You can take five showers, comb your hair nineteen times, open all the windows on this floor, and dawdle till the cows come home, but you'll have to go downstairs eventually.

She paused in front of the bay window next to Rick's armoire. It was warm for March. A gentle breeze carried flower fragrances from their yard below. Rick and Alna planted jonquils, hyacinths, and two forsythia bushes last October, and all were in various stages of bloom. The two of them loved gardening and messing in the dirt. She liked flowers as much as anybody, but she'd just as soon call a landscaper.

Viv breathed in, wanting the floral bouquet below to infuse her with the bravado from last night that escaped her now.

"Mommy?"

She turned to find Alna standing in the doorway.

Alna replaced the gold barrettes with purple ones and pinned her braid up. She experimented more with her hairstyles: a sign her tomboy days were fading. She wore jeans and a purple sweatshirt (both of which would be too short by summer's end).

"Hi, sweetie. Why're you in the doorway like that?"

"Daddy said he thought he heard you. When you didn't come down, I wanted to see if you were okay." She ambled toward Viv, hands in her back pockets. Socks and shoes were probably somewhere in her bedroom, waiting to join the ensemble. Her daughter preferred being barefoot anywhere it was allowed.

"Uh-huh. In other words, you came to tell Mommy to hurry up?"

"Kinda. But, Mommy, where're you goin'? Why you not goin' with me and Daddy?"

"Alna, it's: *Why aren't you going with Daddy and me?* You know how to speak correctly."

"Daddy says I can 'lax the rules when I'm home."

"It's: *re*lax, Alna."

"Okay. But why aren't you going to the fish store with us?"

"Well, who said Mommy wasn't going?" Viv forced a smile instead of biting her bottom lip. *There he goes, taking things to the extreme again.*

"Daddy."

Trying to explain anything to Al was pointless, so Viv let the big picture go and dealt with the matter at hand. "I don't know why Daddy said that, but I'm going."

"Then come on. Daddy's hungry. I had cereal, but I want some eggs." Alna headed for the door. "Can we go by Aunt Louise's? I wa—"

"Al, Mommy needs some Alna-love. You got any?" Viv opened her arms for a hug.

"That's: *do you have* any?" Alna said with a teasing grin. She hugged Viv and kissed her cheek before grasping her hand.

They headed downstairs together.

Rick sat on a barstool at the island counter, reading the newspaper. Viv's habit of reading the newspaper faded over the years since graduate school; she hardly looked at one these days. Rick encouraged Al to read at least four articles of interest weekly.

Sunlight poured into the kitchen from the vast windows in the adjoining family room and sunroom. Located toward the back of the house, their kitchen (decorated in apple green, dark brown, and white) was bright and airy, yet picture-perfect in its coziness. Appliances didn't clutter the granite countertops. Only a laptop, Rick's juice machine (one he insisted on having for Father's Day two years ago but rarely used), and a Crock-Pot were visible. Miniature woodwork carvings, most of which Viv made herself, adorned the counters instead. After their workroom, it was her favorite room in the house.

However, the cozy atmosphere of the kitchen didn't ease the tension created by her earlier request to talk to Rick. Alna, spurred on by excitement over getting new goldfish, innocently served as facilitator at breakfast with her chatter.

Sitting at the table, Viv focused on Rick now and then, but he gave no notice. She also watched her daughter (as Alna switched subjects) and marveled at the miracle of human reproduction.

Alna's hair, redder in her infancy and toddlerhood, was now a warm brown like her father's and complemented her cinnamon-brown complexion (also her father's). A pang of sadness over the loss of her other babies with Rick passed through her core, but she pushed it aside, focusing on her "baby," now nine. Viv saw that, even at nine, Alna inherited her body frame: slender torso and round, shapely hips. Al wouldn't be a string bean all her life; her father's genes lost that battle.

Viv sensed Rick's eyes on her. Awkwardness settled over her heart again as she watched him, instantly and intensely attracted. The way Rick carried himself; to her, he embodied so many grown-ass man qualities. She wanted to jump his bones right there, but changed her line of thinking.

Her attraction to him reached beyond his striking looks; his mind and heart greatly appealed to her.

Other than past indiscretions still painful in the present, she didn't have a long checklist of things wrong with her marriage. But in recent years, aspects of Rick's personality no longer meshed with hers. Complacency had infiltrated. Last night, he exposed a former wild side she remembered fondly and responded to immediately—but doubted she'd see again.

Alna began clearing the table.

"Mommy and Daddy need to talk, honey. Go put something on those stinky feet, then chill in your room awhile, okay?"

Viv expected protest, but Al shrugged and went on her way.

She sensed Rick staring at her again. She stared back.

He lifted his hand to trace that scar on his ear. Irritation etched his handsome features. "So, is this where you finish what you were saying last night? *For real* this time?"

"What do you mean, 'for real this time'?"

"Nothing, Vivian, just go ahead."

She took a breath. "Rick, you know how I love you and Aln—"

"Leave Al out of this."

"Fine." She stared at the almost-empty carafe of orange juice. "...Anyway, I think I need a break from us for a little while. I haven't been happy for some time now..." That was only partly true, so Viv didn't know how to continue. She foresaw doing more hedging. Rick's combative posture provided the gumption she needed to get it out. "I figure Alna and I can stay with Lou and Tim for a few weeks until I find a place. They're close by, so Al's routine won't be interrupted. This way, we can maintain close contact while sorting this out."

Rick stared at her, rubbing his scar, the blaze in his irises simmering. The seconds of silence stretched, and his reticence hurt.

So, she wanted to hurt him. She sat taller, drew her shoulders back. "Also,...I've been seeing Jonathan for the last seven months."

Requesting a separation, coupled with revealing her involvement with Jonathan, should have sent him into spasms of anger. Rick never struck her or even grabbed her as intimidation, and he grew calmer, quieter, with increasing ire. But given his perception of family and loyalty to it, Viv still expected a fist slammed against the table at the very least.

"Wanna go to Columbia Mall or Annapolis Mall? You feel like a ride? It's a good day for it." His warm tone didn't match the stony glint in his eyes, and that tone echoed almost a whisper (his "pissed" trademark). The red in his irises sharpened—another longtime indicator of his seethe. Rick's placid composure said everything, but his casual question threw her.

She sat in disbelief. "Columbia Mall is fine."

Rick issued his customary terse nod. "Done. At the truck in ten." He headed for the foyer.

"Oh, Rick: Al wants to stop by Louise's..." She heard the timidity in her voice, but Rick's reaction threw her.

"Whatever. That's fine." He dashed up the stairs. It sounded like he took two at a time.

She needed to go upstairs, too, but waited, mentally replaying their discussion, before chalking up Rick's response to simple shock.

He wants to finish enjoying this family time with Alna. If he's going to be this rational about it, maybe our separation won't be a last step but a healthy break.

A week later, Viv sat alone at a table on the third tier of DeTante's. She watched Alna, Jonathan, and others strolling the restaurant, viewing the new photos decorating the walls.

Her enthusiasm about their pictures being on display waned, but seeing the absolute joy on her daughter's face delighted her.

Al looked a doll in her skirt and blouse—her hair styled with a bun atop her head. She appeared to be having a ball and acted quite the charmer (from what Viv could tell).

Viv wished Rick had attended but understood his position and didn't press it. She didn't have to make excuses for his absence, but she wanted him there.

Uh, Breaking News: You just told the man you're seeing somebody he knows and that you want out. Even Rick, devoted family man that he is, has his limits.

She returned her attention to the activity below.

DeTante's decor coincided with the change of season. Gone were the dark hues of fall and winter. Viv favored fall and winter, but the restaurant was alive with the symbols of spring.

It was early evening. Although closed to the public, DeTante's bustled with Jonathan's friends, colleagues, and the other photographers whose works were on display.

Viv moved to an empty table after dinner, bringing her water and their belongings. Her seat allowed her view of everything—including everyone's gracious host.

Jonathan held Alna's hand while talking to two young men. He wasn't partial to suits (claiming they emphasized his height), but he wore one this evening: an olive-green suit with a cream-colored shirt and a gold-and-olive-flecked necktie. His shirt and ebony skin presented a favorable contrast. He caught her eye and smiled.

Viv smiled back, her mind somehow on Rick's preference for white dress shirts.

Engrossed in the activity below, she felt a small kiss on her shoulder. Startled, the kiss instantly irritated (embarrassed?) her. She checked if anyone spied the kiss—especially Alna.

"You know better. Where's Alna? I saw her with you a minute ago." Viv scanned DeTante's for her daughter.

Jonathan sat opposite her, turning sideways to allow his legs to extend into the aisle. "Alna's fine. She's with Jo in the kitchens, helping her go over inventory for tomorrow's courses."

"This turned out well, Jon. Alna's going to want to come here more than ever."

"Why're you up here, Viv? You might as well not have come."

Viv sighed, "I know." They were basically alone on tier three (the few others watched the guests' activity on the main floor). Subtle sounds of New Age music drifted around them.

"Having second thoughts?" He wore L'Eau d'Issey. Viv was used to smelling the citrusy spices on Rick; she didn't know why she bought the same for Jonathan.

Or maybe she did. "Yes, and no."

"You wanna break that down for a brutha?"

"What, Jon? You think I'm supposed to be gung-ho about all this? Well, I was at first. Ready to leave Rick and move on. Ready to do the whole sistah-empowered-with-attitude thing. Until I found myself explaining a very adult situation to my nine-year-old daughter. So, now I'm at 'yes and no.' Get it?"

"Got it." His skin was dark, but his eyes were hazel. Even with eyeglasses, his direct gaze made him appear alien under the new lighting. The slightest twinkle of vulnerability in his eyes helped soften his stare and lessened its intensity.

"So, there it is."

Jonathan sat back. "There it is."

"Your turn." Viv reached for her water. Water was about all she could stomach these days—and even that was iffy. Must be the turn of events upsetting her system.

"My turn, what?"

"I broke it down for you. Now tell me, what's on your mind?"

"Well, I'm at 'yes and no,' too." He tapped the table with two rather bony fingers; he had such narrow hands.

"You don't have any major decision-making to do. How can you be at 'yes and no, too'?" Viv sat forward. Since telling Rick she wanted a break, he'd virtually said nothing to her about it (except for telling her in no uncertain terms that Alna wasn't going anywhere); she needed a fight. Jonathan, given their situation, was fair game. "Please break it down for a sistah."

Jonathan leaned forward, too. "So, since I'm the unattached male here, I should have no worries? I should be fine just hittin' that ass?" The intensity in his eyes returned. "You should know me better than that."

Viv did know better. She gazed through the windows.

Late evening crept in as the dusky blue-gray of day transitioned into the twilit purple-blue of night. The lights dimmed gradually. DeTante's famous flutes began their aria.

"Viv?" He waved a hand in front of her face.

She ignored his hand for a few seconds before returning her gaze to him. "Shouldn't you be saying goodnight to your guests?"

"My guests are fine." He sat back with a rolling sigh. "Look, Viv, I'm not married with children. Well, I'm divorced with a teenage son, but he's with his mother, so I'm removed from the day-to-day aspect of raising him. So, no, I don't have the same considerations you do."

"Exactly."

"Hold on now. I do, however, *like* your husband, which doesn't make this easy. Not only that, I have, or thought I had, strong views about the importance of the Black family."

"Meaning?" Viv knew these things, but the fight in her was gone.

"Meaning, I don't want to jeopardize a strong family relationship. Your daughter is innocent here. Rick, too. They haven't done anything to me." He looked away briefly before meeting her eyes again. "So, it's fucked up because I've fallen in love with you, nonetheless."

"I still have the bigger fish to fry, Jon."

"I get that. Just understand, there are Black men with hearts and feelings out here." He paused. "Can I ask something?"

"Sure." Viv finished her water, detecting a subtle aftertaste of copper which produced an iffy moment: more nausea fluttered through.

"When your mind goes through whatever it thinks on when you're trying to figure this thing out, am I in the equation at all?"

Viv rolled her eyes upward with a sigh.

"No, come on now, hear me out. Would you still be leaving Rick if I weren't a part of things?"

"I guess."

"Not good enough."

"I'm sorry?"

"Don't you see? This can't be about you and me, only about you and Rick. And even that must be an absolute—no guessing."

Viv contemplated Jonathan's words while checking the restaurant for her daughter. Alna now helped Jorge reset some tables on tier two. Viv took reluctant seconds before returning her attention to Jonathan; they were now alone on tier three.

"Let me ask this, then, Viv. Do you love me?" His voice cracked on *me*, but his gaze remained direct and purposeful.

"Sure." And she did—just not the way Jonathan meant it. Viv shifted in her seat.

Their table was not in disarray. There wasn't much on the table: cloth napkins, Viv's empty glass, Alna's small purse, a previous occupant's half-full glass of water, and a DeTante's menu.

Viv offered Jonathan a facsimile of a smile and began straightening the table. She placed Alna's purse beside hers in the chair next to her, then adjusted the menu and refolded the napkins, arranging them both just so. The glass of water on her right, Viv moved to her farther right—diligent work.

Jonathan kept quiet as she went about it.

"...You said this can't be about us. That it must be about Rick and me."

"Right."

"Well, this is about me. Rick is content, having no desire to, as he calls it, 'betray our family.' On the other hand, I find myself wanting out—at least for a little while."

Jonathan shook his head and sat back.

"What?"

"Nothing. Never mind. Finish."

"No. You're shaking your head for some reason."

"I'll tell you what's wrong with what you said, but first, I'm going to ask something you never give a straight answer to. Why're you so unhappy with Rick? Why do you want to leave him?"

Viv grew warm.

Someone's glass of water was on the table. Remnants of ice cubes, the size of dimes, floated in it. Despite the iffy effects from water (or anything lately), the water looked good. Viv's throat clicked. She tried picturing who left the glass, attempting the impossible and incredible task of determining whether she should sip the water. Jonathan's question unnerved her; she was that tempted to drink from a stranger's glass.

She cleared her throat. "If you want specifics, Jon, I can't give them."

"So, you don't know."

"No. I know." She just didn't want to discuss it.

Jonathan leaned forward again. "Okay, no specifics then. Try some general reasons. Because I can't recall you giving any of those, either."

She folded her arms across her chest and sucked her teeth, not in the mood for this Oprah moment.

"Why is this so hard for you? You say you want out of your marriage but won't, or can't, pinpoint why. Do you still love the man?"

"Yes."

"Well, that was quick and definitive. Fine. Do you still want him?"

Viv checked that glass out again. "...Most times."

He chuffed a muted snort. "I need some help here, Viv, because I must be missing something. You love and still want him, yet you're determined to leave him." He sat back, amusement in his hazel eyes.

"As I've said, there's no *one* thing, but for now, let's say I'm bored and need a change. Now, why were you shaking your head?"

"You're kidding, right?"

"About what? Needing a change? No."

"What're you doing with me, Viv?"

"Doing with you?" Viv eyeballed the glass again: the ice deserted her.

"You're too old to play games."

"I'm not playing any games."

"Yes, you are. Maybe not intentionally, but you are. And maybe *games* isn't the best word here." He removed his glasses and swiveled his legs under the table. "You say you want out for a brief period. You love him, still want hi—"

"I said, *most times* I want him."

"Amounts to the same. Anyway, all that says to me is I'm a temporary diversion from your 'boring' marriage." He leaned forward, forcing his following words between clenched teeth. "If that is how you see me, then we need to let this thing go—because my feelings for you aren't temporary."

"You're not a passing fling, Jon. Why're you so angry?"

He spewed a short exhale and sat back again. "Because the only reason you can give for leaving your marriage is boredom. What kind of shit is that? You're bored? Rick's boring? So, you need a change? That's weak, Viv. Weak and sad."

"Weak or not, it's the truth, Jon."

"Then stay with Rick. You don't break up a family because you're bored. I should be hearing something about adultery, refusal to work and contribute to the household, verbal or physical abuse—something concrete. I mean, okay, you're 'bored.' Does that mean I'll be a distant memory once you're bored with me?"

She could have mentioned Rick cheating, but didn't want to. Besides, she understood why Rick—

"I do love you," she said at a higher volume than intended, but she wanted him to hear her say it.

"And you love Rick?"

"I do. Yes." Once again, the declaration warmed her.

Jonathan observed her in silence before brushing his slacks with his palms and straightening his tie. He stood and leaned over, lightly kissing her forehead. His cologne again reminded her of Rick. "Look. This is supposed to be a joyous occasion. It's not like we're going to solve anything tonight. I need to check in downstairs, being the host and all."

Viv suddenly realized how tired she was. "Okay."

He nodded and started away, stretching his neck before heading down to the main level.

Viv reflected on their conversation, on the unsettled atmosphere in her home. The tension at home proved a bit much sometimes, but she didn't know what else to do. Admittedly, she and Rick were handling Alna's situation well; both were determined to keep her stress to a minimum. They remained, if not overly amiable, at least polite, during the only real time they spent together these days—dinnertime (a ritual kept in place for their daughter's sake).

Rick was a homebody nowadays, mainly wanting to venture out as a family. She thought recent developments would've sparked a change in him. Maybe he'd stay away from the house out of anger or, if nothing else, try to make her curious about his comings and goings.

Rick seemed bent on maintaining his presence at home. An unvoiced challenge, but Viv did what she knew best: ignored him.

Instead of going to Louise's, she moved into a spare bedroom while Rick stayed in the primary. That wasn't the way she wanted things, but Rick pointed out she was the one talking separation; Viv supposed it was fair enough. Since she only halfheartedly searched for another place to live, the current sleeping arrangement served its purpose.

There'd been no confrontations since their argument about Alna going with her. Aside from the staid (but cordial) ambiance at the dinner table, communication hovered around nil. Viv was relieved at the minimal drama, but part of her wanted to say *something* to him. They were friends, Rick, her buddy, so it was suddenly a strange situation. Although she'd never admit it, the tension was getting to her.

Tired of thinking, she just wanted to go home. Regardless of the disruption in her life, she loved her house and wanted to be in it. She and Rick no longer shared a bedroom (another strange situation), but Viv used their garden whirlpool tub with robust enthusiasm. A relaxing session in that tub beckoned.

She stared through DeTante's upper windows, trying to "read" the time, as her husband often did so well. After a minute or two of trying to determine the time by surveying the sky like Rick, Viv gave up. Essentially, the purple-blue sky with its streaky clouds told her it was night and later than six o'clock. *Rick would know the time within a fifteen-minute window.* It was one of his endearing quirks.

Jonathan returned, but they sat in silence.

"You ready to head down?" Viv added the last three words to that question with minuscule delay. Jonathan knew nothing about the double entendre of *You ready?* (that she and Rick shared), but still.

"Might as well. But let me say this. Just because I want you to be sure about things has nothing to do with how I feel about you or change my wanting to be with you. Love doesn't work like that."

"You sure are tossing the love word around."

"Yeah. Ain't love grand?" He wore the biggest smile.

Viv smiled back.

How could she not, with him gleaming like that? She smiled warmly, but a small glacier eased into the pit of her stomach. Jonathan's reply reminded her of the dream about the faceless women. Although every detail remained fresh, she had yet to analyze it. "I guess it is."

Catching movement out of the corner of her eye, she glanced over in time to spot Alna heading into the kitchens. Viv gathered their things and headed down (giving a last glance at the stranger's glass of water).

When they reached DeTante's main level, Alna was behind her, sitting at a table—and eating again. "Hi, Mommy!"

Jonathan moseyed toward the bar.

"Hey, Al. Ready to go?"

"Okay." Alna stood. Besides a tiny spot on her collar, she looked as neat and clean as she did before leaving home. *Yep, she's growing up.* They walked to the bar to say their goodbyes to Jonathan and Rosie (engaged in murmuring chatter).

"Well, that's it for us. We're outta here." Viv was sure she sounded too nonchalant—and too loud, given the restaurant's quiet atmosphere.

"Did you enjoy yourself, Alna?" Jonathan leaned on the counter, one foot resting on the brass footrail. He looked nice.

Is love fun? Viv dismissed the thought.

Alna grinned. "Yes."

Glimpsing the new pictures, Viv noticed those belonging to her and Alna. "Thank you, Jonathan, for making us a part of this."

"Oh, almost forgot." Jonathan leaned over the bar to Rosie's side, craning his neck to view the shelving underneath. He extended his right arm. "Rosie, can you hand me that envelope?" Following Jonathan's reach and gaze, Rosie retrieved a manila envelope from under the bar and handed it to him. He handed Viv the envelope, who accepted it with a questioning dented brow and wrinkled nose.

Alna gripped her forearm with both hands. "What is it, Mommy?"

Viv used her sense of touch to determine the contents. "I think these are our leftover pictures, sweetie." She peeked under the envelope's flap. "Yep. See?" She gave Alna a better look.

"Can we put these up at home?"

"Sure. We'll go shopping for frames this weekend. Now, tell Mister Rast and Rosie 'thank you,' so we can go."

"Thank you, Mister Rast. Thanks, Rosie," Alna recited, sounding much like fourth graders greeting their teachers in class.

Viv leaned to give Jonathan the customary oh-we're-just-platonic-friends kiss on the cheek. He turned toward her, causing their faces to graze. Eight fifty-one p.m. shadow speckled his face; he needed to shave. His cologne and the roughness of his cheek made Viv think of more intimate things. She pulled away from Jonathan and waved goodbye to Rosie.

Once home, with Alna settled, Viv pursued a deep, hot bubble bath. Once submerged, she waited for her skin to stop tingling from the water's heat. Tension resulting from her conversation with Jonathan, the awkward atmosphere at home, and the day's activity, dissolved with the soft, crackling sound of the bubbles popping.

The hot water soothed her body, but Viv's nerves remained on edge. She tittered quietly, believing a cold shower would be better in her current state.

Usually, a hot bath or good sex took the edginess out of her irritable moods. The latter was out, but the tub wasn't doing its job—and giving herself some personal attention just would not cut it. The whole predicament struck her as funny.

Although she was horny from interaction with Jonathan, fuck the dumb stuff: she wanted Rick. Her husband's body, his skill with hers, always left her panting and moaning deep with gratification.

Viv squeezed a quarter-sized dollop of liquid soap onto her body sponge. She lathered and washed twice, trying to keep her mind occupied with what she was doing and thoughts away from what she *wanted* to be doing (with Rick).

If I continue with this situation much longer, I'll go nuts.

She was used to getting some whenever the mood struck her. But although she was "with" Jonathan, she wasn't *with* him, so he wasn't available on the regular. And although Rick was available, he wasn't "available," so her options (suddenly) had become limited.

Done bathing, she got out of the tub and toweled off.

Securing her robe around her, she cracked the bathroom door, and listened. The sound of something hitting the kitchen floor (and Rick's "*Cazzo!*") told her Rick was still downstairs.

Viv hurried back to "her" bedroom.

Opting to sleep in lounge pants and one of Rick's T-shirts, she climbed into the queen-sized bed, pulled the comforter over her shoulders, and fell asleep.

Chapter 4

Three's a Crowd

Rick sat on the hood of his black Range Rover, gazing at the budding greenery of the trees, and humming.

He'd been coming to the park, sitting on the hood of his truck, and humming oldies every day for the past week. He liked today's music well enough, but the often-sampled soul and R&B from the 1960s and 1970s trumped the current stuff.

And music by Earth, Wind & Fire? Nothing like it.

Right now, "Zoom" by the Commodores felt good in his throat.

Viv's announcement shattered his world almost two weeks ago, but he couldn't come to terms with it.

She hadn't left, deciding to stay in a spare bedroom instead, and he didn't know if that was helping matters or hurting them. Oh, he nipped her idea of taking Alna with her in the bud—and left it up to Viv to explain everything to their daughter.

Mainly, though, he wanted to hit her.

Just punch her in the face with everything he had. That embodied the extent of his anger, but he would never strike her. So, he ventured to the park, humming tunes until he felt better.

Most times, the humming worked. The times it didn't, left him thinking too much, "seeing" too much. It was his imagination, the "seeing," that curdled his stomach, made him ill with—many things not good.

He slid off the hood and ambled toward the lake, gathering rocks along the way and stuffing them into his pockets. The overcast late-afternoon sky contributed to the slight chill in the air. Only a handful of people strolled about. He guessed there would be more activity after Easter, but the clouds and the relative isolation complemented his frame of mind.

At the lake's ridge, Rick removed the rocks from his pockets, forming a pile by his foot, then stood on the bank, watching the water.

He *knew* something was off at dinner with her that night; before Rast joined them, sure—but even more once Rast came. He sensed that shit.

Jaw tightening, he thought about Alna's sad little face when she came in with Viv from their visit to Zibby's Fun Palace. Since he opted out, Viv chose that opportunity to broach the subject of the separation—and Rick hated her for it.

Although she did the right thing by leaving Jonathan out of her explanation, she chose a time and place that should have been tied to pleasant *family* memories.

He was in the kitchen when they returned. Seeing Alna's confusion and sadness, he seriously considered striking Viv then. Instead, he gathered his daughter in his arms while Viv stood in the laundry room doorway. Alna never cried but asked a straightforward question, muffled by his shoulder: *"What happened, Daddy?"*

The silence after that question echoes in my home.

Because Viv wouldn't answer the question—and he couldn't.

Rick now hummed Earth, Wind & Fire's "Keep Your Head to the Sky." He threw rocks into the water, reflecting on the unwelcome turmoil at home. He'd said little to Viv about her request to separate. He knew it bothered her, but he didn't intend to say much because, truthfully, there wasn't much to say.

If she's decided to abandon their family, he wasn't go'n help her feel better about it. Basic math.

He wasn't as upset with Rast as he expected, which surprised him. Oh, Rast was a bastard for pulling up on his wife, and he intended to tell him so (although words may not suffice). But ultimately, it rested with Viv's decision to betray their family.

He considered Viv wanting payback for his past indiscretions.

Okay, whatever. I would never leave my family.

Rick launched stones onto the opposite bank, throwing them harder, farther. The force behind his throws soon wrenched his left shoulder. He ignored the pain. Each throw buoyed his resolve: Viv wasn't going anywhere. With each throw, he felt better.

A dark cloud of emotion—something stranger but more comforting than anger—solidified in his middle.

He paused, surveying the sky for the time: around five forty-five p.m. Dinnertime. Regardless of recent developments, he and Viv maintained the routine. It was his turn to cook. Tired and achy, he headed home to his wife and child—his family.

Rick loved his neighborhood: colonial homes perched on well-kept lawns. The glowing streetlights broadcast an unsettled luster as nightfall edged closer.

He pulled into the garage (parking next to Viv's pearl-gray Lexus GS350), killed the ignition, and waited.

He didn't know whether to enter the laundry room as usual or through the front door. Entering through the front door made it less likely he'd interact with her if she was in the kitchen or family room.

Pissed over the idea of walking around on eggshells, he got out of his SUV and entered the laundry room.

He braced for a curt "Hello" and a dash toward the stairs, but when he entered the kitchen, Viv could be heard but not seen. She set the alarm to bypass, so it didn't beep. The television was off, but the radio provided background noise. It was mostly dark. A lamp in the sunroom was on, and the pilot glowed on the stove's right back burner, a large pot sitting on its eye.

Rick didn't know Viv's exact whereabouts, so he listened for several seconds. Her voice came from the sunroom. He doubted she heard him come in.

He stood in the kitchen, contemplating what to fix for dinner. He wanted to peek inside the pot but feared any sound the top made as he returned it might alert Viv to his presence; right now, he was glad she didn't know he was home.

We'll have baked chicken and seasoned wild rice. I'm not in the mood for anything elaborate.

For a vegetable, Rick decided on corn. He hated vegetables, but he suffered through downing them for Alna's sake. Because of its sweet taste, corn proved easier to roll with than many other greens and yellows, so the kid in him preferred it.

Quick-and-easy dinner decided, he wanted to shower first; hot water on his shoulder would help the tenderness. He turned for the stairs but hesitated, hearing Viv's voice from the sunroom. She was on the phone.

His heartbeat picked up. He rubbed sweaty palms on his jeans, feeling like a criminal in his own home. And like a criminal, he tiptoed from the kitchen into the family room, staying as close to the shadows as possible. He eavesdropped on his wife's end of the conversation.

"Uh-huh," Viv said.

Silence.

"No, Friday is better. Being a dress-down day and all."

He heard strains of a voice coming through the receiver.

"He didn't say."

Silence.

Viv sighed. "I haven't figured that part out yet."

Rick retreated, heading for the front of the house and upstairs, figuratively patting himself on the back for his proactive thinking.

That awful day, when Viv announced wanting to separate, Rick held his tongue, but his mind worked far ahead. After he asked Viv about the choice of malls for their outing, he went upstairs to the smallest spare bedroom and retrieved an old telephone from the walk-in closet. He was thankful he didn't get rid of it (despite Viv's protestations). The royal-blue rotary-dial phone (he "borrowed" from his parents) was a throwback from his college days.

That awful day (guided by a wily sense of need), Rick retrieved the phone. He unscrewed the mouthpiece and removed the circular voice transmitter (a trick Dave showed him). Phone back in the closet, he took his family to the mall.

That move weeks ago served him now.

Twilight coming through the upstairs windows illuminated the upper floor. Alna was in her room, so Rick tipped into the spare bedroom Viv didn't occupy and closed the door. After retrieving the phone from the closet and plugging it in the wall jack, he cautiously lifted the receiver and listened.

"—times do I have to explain this?" Viv sounded hurt.

"I'm just wondering about your motives, Viv." It was Louise.

"My motives are fine, Lou. It's funny. I've been thinking about my mother more. Maybe she's messaging me to go with how I'm feeling."

"Viv, I'm not trying to be mean. I didn't know your mom, but that sounds like a bunch of bull. Next week is the twenty-fifth anniversary of her death. *That's* why she's been on your mind."

Silence.

Rick half-expected Viv to hang up with an attitude.

"So, what's this: your Vietnamese wisdom coming through?"

Both women chuckled.

"Maybe. Still, you have to get at why you're leaving Rick."

Rick gripped the phone tighter.

Louise continued: "If you're bored and want Rick to recapture how he was, until what, two, three years ago, say that. If it's worrying about him cheating again, then say that. If you worry about having another baby, tell Rick that. Just quit with the abstract, mystical shit. After fifteen years of marriage, Rick deserves better—and so does your mother."

"I can't compartmentalize and sum my unhappiness into one reason, Lou. It's a combination of things."

Louise released a lengthy exhale. "I'm tired of talking about this. You know how I feel about what you're doing. But you're my girl, so I'm here for you. Anyway, what time Friday are you meeting Jonathan?"

"Around ten-fifteen."

"Why so early?"

"He has a meeting at one."

"What're you telling Rick?"

"I'm not 'telling' him anything. Why?"

"Well, what if he calls or something?"

"Rick rarely calls during the morning while we're at work. Besides, that's what voicemail is for."

"I'm not feeling this, Viv. Why can't you be honest? You said he knows about Jonathan."

"I know, but... Anyway, Missus Louise Nguyễn-Collins, get off my phone. I'm tired of talking about this myself. Oh, can you see Alna tomorrow afternoon? She's complaining about a toothache, but I think she wants to talk, especially since you checked her teeth last month."

"Yeah, Al needs to talk to somebody, you need to talk to somebody, and Rick probably needs to get some things off his chest. I've mentioned this before, but why don't you give Doctor Alexander a call? Naomi's a good family therapist, Viv."

Silence from Viv. But Rick, intrigued, wanted to know more.

Louise sighed. "Tomorrow's fine. Any time after five, okay?"

"No problem. We'll talk tomorrow. Bye."

"Bye." Louise hung up first.

Viv hung up.

Rick made sure the ladies disconnected before hanging up. It pleased him to hear Louise wasn't entirely in Viv's corner.

Using his shirttail, Rick wiped the receiver down (no idea why). He then unplugged the phone and returned it to the closet, placing it next to the gun box on the shelf. He did all this calmly enough; that much more determined, Viv wasn't breaking up their family.

Somebody's life depended on it.

Giving the gun box a final sideways glance (that Smith & Wesson 9mm needed to go back into their bedroom), he hurried to their bedroom for a shower.

Viv spoke few words at dinner, but Rick was a virtual chatterbox. While teasing Al at the table, he sometimes glanced at Viv: a tentative smile played around her mouth. That was fine, but he'd call her Friday morning, anyway.

Friday evening, Rick sat in the sitting room waiting.

A door slammed downstairs several minutes ago.

He didn't care if she was pissed. After what she'd done to their family, pissing her off was the least he could do.

Hearing Viv ascending the stairs, he picked up his tablet computer and reclined on the leather loveseat.

"Rick?!"

Yeah, she was miffed. "In here."

Viv entered their sitting room. "Was that necessary, Rick?"

He continued surfing the web. "Beg pardon? Was *what* necessary?"

"Was calling my office and cell, leaving *eleven* messages necessary? You know what I'm talking about."

"Why didn't you call back?"

"I don't know. You barely left a message, didn't text. I thought—"

"Yes," he interrupted, knowing why she didn't call back, but determined to keep his tone devoid of emotion.

"Yes, what?"

"Calling that many times was necessary."

"...Why?" She now sounded puzzled, her anger seeming to dissipate.

He put his tablet down. "To talk. We've been together too long for this to be over after one conversation. That's not happening, Vivian. You and Alna mean more to me than you'll ever understand."

"I do understand, Rick. But as much as I love Alna, this is for me. And I love you, Rick. I've tried—"

"Tried *what*, Viv?" He swung his legs around and faced her.

She looked lovely in her denim jeans and black form-fitting sweater. Her slender waist and those shapely hips said, *female*. Some earthy tone on her lips complemented her butterscotch-caramel skin. Thankfully, Viv mainly limited her cosmetics to shaded lip gloss; she didn't need makeup. And even from a distance, her inky jet irises (however cold and unfriendly in the moment) ruled him.

A whiff of her camellia-sandalwood body oil came his way, creating subtle, arousing distraction. She did well blending many natural fragrances for her range of body-oil combos, from varied florals and spices to sandalwood, jasmine, vanilla, and moss.

He stayed focused. "Instead of coming to me when you started having these feelings, you let them build until you wanted out. You didn't give me a chance to fix it." He shook his head and stood. "No, Viv, you haven't 'tried.' You haven't tried at all." He strode past her, gritting his teeth and fighting the desire to grab his gorgeous wife and kiss her deeply, making all this horrible bullshit go away.

"So now you're going somewhere to pout? After calling me over ten times within three hours today and leaving a cryptic non-message, now you walk away?"

Rick turned to her. She looked close to crying, but he knew better. "That's pretty much what you did. Just 'walked away'?" He continued toward the stairs without looking back. "But no, pouting is not what I intend to do. And I'm not giving up on our marriage either, Vivian. It's as simple as that."

"It's not like you haven't done your share o' shit!"

He continued down the stairs, letting the silence speak for him.

Rick went to the basement. Their furnished basement, decorated with themes of learning and science, never became as cozy as other rooms.

Because no one spends time down here.

The basement wasn't where he wanted to be. He headed back up the stairs. He needed to think and did his best thinking while in motion. The workroom would be his best bet; he could work on his cars.

Since he and Viv pursued hobbies requiring special tools and space, they added the workroom adjoining the garage several years ago. Viv enjoyed woodworking and created anything from decorative miniature pieces to the various moderate pieces of furniture placed throughout their home.

His interest was model cars: a hobby initially his brother's. When his father started boxing up David's things for charity, Rick claimed the model cars. He had difficulty accepting David's leaving, so the connection to his brother remained sacred.

Rick entered their workroom, immediately assaulted by the redolence of acrylic and smoky sawdust. He stood in the doorway, scanning the space: a sizable, almost-perfect square. The room was never officially divided into his-side-her-side, but a natural separation of territories was evident. Viv performed her usual cleanup after woodworking a few days ago, but traces of sawdust persisted, invading his side.

Rick went to his side, staring at the mess that was his worktable. As of late, he concentrated his efforts on a 1967 Ford Mustang. No surprise there. He loved Mustangs. Dave had been partial to Chevys, but since taking over the hobby, the number of Mustang models outnumbered everything else.

Rick sat on his stool, rotating side to side. The Mustang needed the excess glue and plastic trimmed before priming could begin. He picked up his blade and got to work.

He trimmed, thinking about colors for his car. Trimmed and contemplated calling the family therapist Louise mentioned.

What was her name again? Oh yeah, Dr. Alexander. Dr. Naomi Alexander.

Rick worked on the Mustang for an hour.

In the end, he decided metallic brown would be best, and he would contact this Dr. Alexander by himself before bringing his family to her. He needed to get with Louise anyway if he was to uncover any good information about Viv.

Louise would tell him. Her loving him all the wrong ways for years would be enough to get her talking.

He also wanted to talk to Rast. Make it clear: three was a crowd. But that could wait.

Rick stood and stretched, examining his latest work.

She was ready for coat one, but later. He wanted to make a phone call and grab a snack, but first, he needed to see a man about a horse.

Rick left the workroom for the bathroom, whistling his rendition of Earth, Wind & Fire's "After the Love Has Gone."

He felt better than he had in weeks. And between Louise and Dr. Alexander, Rick hoped to be feeling even better soon.

Chapter 5

Moody Blue

D r. Naomi Alexander sat across from her patient (a woman having severe issues with her sister), wanting nothing more than to go home. Go home and have a Hennessy Sidecar (prepared with X.O.) served in a coupe glass. Nevertheless, she assumed the concerned-and-attentive-psychiatrist pose and let the woman, Willette Hargrove, finish her session. Willette had twelve minutes left, so Naomi tried giving her full attention to those twelve minutes.

Willette didn't speak for eight long minutes, her facial expression changing with the apparent dialogue going on in her head.

Naomi leaned back in her chair.

Maybe white wine would be better. I have two reviews due tomorrow. Yes, a few Cerignola olives and some chardonnay while listening to some Joseph Bologne (Chevalier) sounded ideal. Perhaps two of his violin concertos: Violin Concerto No.1 in C major, Op. 5, and Violin Concerto No. 2 in A minor, Op. 5.

"Envious, I guess," Willette said, interrupting Naomi's thoughts.

Naomi scratched her eyebrow and stared at her patient. Eight minutes—and that's *all* she comes back with? "Willette, have you voiced anything *new* here? You've spent weeks trying to get across how you're *not* jealous of your sister." She stood.

Willette took the hint and prepared to leave, stuffing her photo album companion back into her carryall.

"Look, Willette." Naomi resumed business mode. She limited her professional posture with her patients; the stance wasn't conducive to getting them to open up. But she was irritated now, not as interested in

Willette opening up. "The session is over, but let's have a better answer next week."

Willette's eyes quavered before she nodded.

Naomi headed to her desk. "Then I'll see you next Monday. At three rather than four. Okay?" She removed her eyeglasses, placing them on her desk with a click.

She watched Willette leave her office. The woman habitually wore very loose, ill-fitting clothes. Her charcoal-gray two-piece outfit hung about her like the skin on an elephant having lost too much weight. Naomi trained to mind the details, so she observed how Willette's backside rounded the sides of the skirt, how her breasts did the same for the top.

You'd have to wear a muumuu to cover all you want to hide, my dear girl; too-large outfits won't cut it.

Naomi needed to call her daughter Leslie. She reached for the phone as the door closed, seeing her message light.

It can wait till tomorrow.

But Naomi didn't pick up the receiver to call Leslie. She stared at the tiny red rectangle winking at her.

Intuition. A hunch. Naomi called the sensation now passing through her a "flash of truth." And, at 44, she was virtually unaffected by its occurrence, having lived with the "flashes" (and the "aura-flickers") for over twenty years.

She was a sophomore in college when she experienced her first flash. It helped her decide between either astronomy or psychiatry as her major. She happened to be peeing at the time.

Her first aura-flicker occurred weeks later. And even though she didn't know what was happening, she paid attention to it and was all the better for it when dealing with an incognito racist professor. Naomi still remembered the unsettledness stirring her middle upon seeing those sudden hues surrounding the professor. Blackish brown shades (hints of dull red and forest-green) shrouded Professor Helman (her cerulean eyes smiling but not) as she attempted to dissuade her from the field of medicine, using all the typical flowery backhanded phrasing.

But that was then. Right now, it was a flash informing her.

Her flashes of truth manifested as acute hunches (often with im-agery) somehow, someway, grounded in truth. And in the twenty-plus years since her first one, the flashes occurred haphazardly at best. The same for her aura-flickers (as one's auras changed as fluidly as day-to-day, month-to-month, year-to-year). She could go weeks, sometimes months, without an occurrence. Naomi didn't question where her flashes and flickers came from, satisfied they didn't happen often. And, although she didn't gamble, the haphazard nature of the hunches didn't provide a financial advantage in making the perfect wager, either.

Naomi didn't put too much paranormal or supernatural stock into the occurrences. Believing herself neither seer nor psychic (and unicorns didn't exist), she told no one about them—not even Tyson. She lived with them, learned what she could about them (chakras, planes, auric bodies), and applied her philosophies regarding whatever she was "seeing." These talents were innate; Naomi didn't train in any form or fashion for this stuff. Some practiced achieving auric sight; she didn't have to. And the irregular infrequency of it all made it simple, easy to manage. She'd never seen her aura—and was thankful for small favors.

Naomi grew still. Less than a minute passed; her flash was over. She picked up the phone and called her daughter. After leaving a voicemail message, she stared at the message light. "I'll speak with him tomorrow."

She knew her encounter with him and the woman he brought (his wife, no doubt) would upset her already-wavering principles yet be galvanizing and entertaining.

The clanging pots and pans rankled her nerves.

It was just shy of five-thirty in the morning. She hadn't fallen asleep until well after two (2:37 a.m. is what Naomi last remembered the clock reading). So, she was beginning another day with less than three hours of sleep. Naomi was used to getting little sleep, but the noise proved too much this morning.

Someone clanged a frying pan onto the stove. Someone else ran water into two enormous pots in the sink, creating a loud (and disturbing) whoosh. Clangs and whooshes. Naomi stiffened but pasted on a smile for Tammy, who filled the pots.

Wasn't it Tuesday two days ago?

Naomi wanted a drink. She thought of the flask of Hennessy X.O. in her briefcase and just as quickly dismissed it. *A homeless shelter, where you've come to help people, is the last place you need to be (seen) drinking.* With a sigh, she steeled herself against the kitchen sounds and continued peeling potatoes and sending them through the slicer.

Every Tuesday for the past nine years, Naomi volunteered to help the less fortunate. Apart from one occasion, she never missed a Tuesday. To spread the love and keep things spicy, Naomi changed her community service effort every eighteen to twenty-four months.

Last May, she started working with Hardluck Rebound, a group of volunteer men and women who rotated preparing meals for the local homeless. The group Naomi signed up for performed charitable service on Tuesdays.

This Tuesday, they were serving breakfast in the cafeteria of a defunct and aging elementary school in northwest DC.

With the potatoes peeled, sliced, and ready for frying, Naomi carried two bowls, heavy with potatoes, over to Merriam, who readied iron skillets. Naomi was a tiny woman, approaching five feet three and a drop above 110 pounds, but she carried the bowls with ease. Setting the bowls on the table, she removed her home-team Baltimore Ravens cap and ran a hand over her close-cropped hair, damp with sweat. She needed to contact her barber soon.

"Probably going to have an early summer," Merriam commented. Gone almost as quickly as it appeared, her aura flickered with shades of pink, yellow, and green (a pleasant mix). Interestingly, she rarely saw "hyper-concentrated" auras (emanating solely from the head, heart, or hip areas, for example); they tended towards whole-body aura-flickers—giving her a glimpse of a person's overall physical-emotional-mental energy state, she guessed.

"You might be right on that one, Miss Merriam." Naomi placed her cap back on her head, backward this time. "For March, it's already warm outside, and it's only going to get warmer in here once we get rolling." She sensed someone approaching before Merriam's gaze shifted, so she turned.

"Horace can't make it today." Leslie hugged her. "But he's sending a stand-in. Hi, Miss Merriam."

Leslie (20) inherited her height from her father, Tyson. His height had whispered over six feet, depending on whom he stood next to, but practically anyone appeared taller standing next to Naomi.

At five feet nine, Leslie drew attention. Her dignified walk only emphasized her height. Even in the sweatpants and T-shirt she wore now, Leslie looked regal. She had plain brown eyes, but her thick, shapely eyebrows complemented her modest nose. With Naomi's mocha-brown complexion, Leslie didn't have a blemish: only the littlest mole in front of her right earlobe.

She only wished Leslie hadn't cut her hair (now close-cropped, too). Naomi still waited for Leslie's new look to grow on her.

Naomi looked up at her daughter. "Didn't think he would from the way he sounded last night. Visiting him later?"

"I thought I might."

"Mmm. Let him know we're thinking of him."

"What, Ma?"

"Not now, Les."

"Yeah, right." Leslie strutted past Naomi to the stove, where she poured cooking oil into the skillets Merriam set aside.

Merriam cleared her throat. She was a large woman with pecan-brown skin who possessed the softest, sweetest voice. "Look, why don't you two finish the potatoes? I'll help Tammy with the grits." She spoke more to Naomi than Leslie, giving Naomi a conspiratorial wink before turning away.

Naomi watched the others working.

Like cogs in a well-oiled machine, everyone moved about the kitchen. They operated at a rhythm that would soon have a hot, hearty breakfast ready for about a hundred people in less than two hours. Naomi watched them with pride.

Somehow, she became the unofficial leader of the Tuesday group. That type of thing happened so regularly she was used to it, but she had no problem removing the "leader" hat and letting it find another owner. Taking one last look at her team of ten (well, nine until Horace's sub arrived), Naomi resumed preparing fried potatoes and onions with her daughter. "You wanna get the rest of the potatoes? I'll slice onion."

"Fine." Leslie walked away.

I am not in the mood for this.

Leslie carried two more bowls filled with pre-prepped potatoes and placed them on the table. "This should be plenty."

Naomi pulled a bag of onions toward them.

"No electric slicer?"

Naomi shook her head. "Not for this."

Leslie peeled onions. Naomi sliced them. They worked in silence.

"...I don't see how you do it," Leslie said.

"My eyes don't water when I'm slicing onion. So?" Cooking-talk was safer ground.

"Well, why didn't I get your impervious-to-onion gene? Or your southpaw one?" Leslie wiped a tear from her cheek.

"You'll have to take that up with a Higher Power. And being left-hand-ed has its drawbacks." Naomi handed Leslie a two-handed scoop of sliced onions. No, her eyes didn't respond to the chemical compound syn-Propanethial-S-oxide. The sulfur-based acids and enzymes didn't affect her eyes the way they did most people. She didn't have to wear goggles, keep onions cold during prep, or use an extra-sharp knife (to reduce the release of enzymes). The onion could be warm and sliced at the root using a butter knife—and her eyes remained as dry as ever while anyone around her wept and wailed. She didn't know what to make of it and didn't care. She didn't cry while slicing raw onion. Moving on. "Here, start with these."

"Ma, the potatoes need to cook some first." Leslie guided her hands back and reached for a bowl of potatoes.

Tammy turned on her portable CD player. Mahalia Jackson's "Upper Room" mingled with the clanging kitchen sounds.

"Got all turned around there for a sec." Naomi stifled a yawn, letting it seep through her lips. "Tired, I guess."

Leslie sent her a sideways glance. "Still not sleeping?"

"It's getting better."

"For a psychiatrist, you sure don't lie very well."

"Shrinks are supposed to be expert liars?" Naomi hurried her slicing; they were falling behind schedule.

"No, but with the mental hijinks you get involved in, surely a white-lie comes into play." Leslie slid two handfuls of potatoes into the oil and added four more. She sighed. "So why don't you want me seeing Ho-race?" The question traveled a modicum above the noise of the kitchen.

"It's not Horace per se, Les. It's Horace, Gavin, Trevor, Clarence. And, oh, what's his name? Adello. I don't understand why you must see so many men."

"*Seeing* them, Ma, not sleeping with them. Well, not *all* of them." Leslie snickered at her correction.

Naomi smirked. "Cute. But I'm still your mother. There's sharing, and then there is TMI."

"Uh-huh. Anyway, I thought you'd like Gavin: he's an artist."

Naomi hesitated. "What's that got to do with anything?"

"Seems it has to do with everything lately."

Naomi did not want to have this conversation.

The women worked together in relative silence.

"...Sorry you feel that way."

Leslie huffed a scoffing puff of air. "You're sorry I haven't followed your advice."

"Oh, so now *you're* the therapist?"

"No, but like you, I just calls 'em as I sees 'em."

"Then why can't you 'see' art as your true calling, not international marketing?" Naomi pulled another bowl of potatoes closer.

"Because I'm practical like Daddy was."

Naomi stiffened. "And practicality kept your father miserable."

"You always say that, but I never saw it."

There was another quiet period of frying potatoes and onions, of transferring cooked potatoes and onions into large aluminum trays. The neutral silence served its calming purpose.

"Les, we often shield children from the negative."

"I was sixteen when Daddy left us, not six. I would have known if Daddy was unhappy."

"First of all, Les, your father died. He didn't 'leave us,' the way you keep saying it. You should be stronger about that now."

"Should be, but I'm not. Second of all?"

"There were plenty signs you didn't notice."

"Such as?"

"Such *as*, you need to turn those potatoes. They're scorching."

"I got this, Ma. Finish." Leslie added more oil to the pan.

"Well, you know how he constantly complained of fatigue and rarely wanted to do anything recreational."

"He was tired."

"Exactly. He worked hard and lost his enthusiasm for much of the goofy stuff in life."

"The 'goofy stuff,' Ma?"

"Yes, the goofy stuff. Look, Les, I had conservative parents, so I appreciate your desire for a conventional plan. But be happy, too."

Leslie added potatoes to a tray. "Studying marketing strategies from varying world views is interesting. I like it."

"Yeah, but when you sculpt, tell the truth: there's nothing like it. Is there?" It surprised Naomi this topic progressed well; angry words were usually spoken by now.

Leslie didn't respond.

"Les...?"

"When the police pulled in front of our house, what went through your mind?" Leslie stood motionless, both hands holding an aluminum tray filled with cooked potatoes.

"Unadulterated curiosity." It was the truth. Naomi avoided recalling that day, but memories have no expiration date.

That Tuesday in late August was muggy, the air damp from thunderstorms the night before. Naomi, Tyson, and Leslie were planting portulaca and waxy begonias in the muddy front yard. It was late in the season, but Naomi didn't care. They purchased the plants a week before, and the plants then sat in the garage most of that time, Naomi only occasionally remembering to give the things some water.

That Tuesday afternoon, they were gardening, but Tyson, in one of his rare moments, had a taste for doughnuts and headed to Dunkin' Donuts with everyone's order. The closest Dunkin' Donuts shop was fifteen minutes away. Tyson left that afternoon around four o'clock.

Afternoon moved into evening as Naomi planted and replanted, paying little attention to the time. Leslie abandoned the activity around six-thirty, content to keep her mother company. For 16, Leslie was quite the conversationalist, so Naomi didn't mind gardening solo.

It was odd (and she has never forgiven herself), but at eight-fifteen, it occurred to her: Tyson wasn't back. It was odd because Tyson wasn't one to take side jaunts when out on an errand; she should have been alarmed long before eight-fifteen. But as involved as she was in the gardening, Naomi hadn't given Tyson another thought.

She started to have Leslie call her father, when a county police car carrying two officers pulled up. Naomi was kneeling in the dirt when the white car (with its familiar stripes and shield) approached, its lights flaring silently. They didn't use the vacant driveway, which struck a chord with her. She remembers standing protectively in front of Leslie, wondering what in the world cops were doing at her house. The idea they might be there because of Tyson never crossed her mind.

They buried Tyson the following Tuesday.

"Why're you asking about that now, Les?" Naomi surveyed the kitchen: everything was ready except the eggs. She started toward where Ben and Vanessa prepped trays of breakfast meats (hoping to swipe a sausage link or two). But a choked sound, low in Leslie's throat, halted her. She turned to her daughter.

"Just am." Leslie stared at her tray of potatoes. "I carry the memory of that day with me, always. But I can never recall how I felt when those policemen came."

"Well, honey, that's—"

Leslie's eyes hardened. "Ma, we're not in 'session' here, okay?"

"I know that."

"Well, I don't want you to—"

"I'm not. Go 'head." Naomi's throat dried up. She and Leslie rarely discussed Tyson's death. She didn't know why her daughter broached the subject now, but there was a reason. The psychiatrist in Naomi allowed her the patience to wait for it.

"All I'm saying is, when I try to conjure how I felt, I'm grasping at straws. I try to feel how I *should've* felt, but it doesn't ring true. The only feeling that does is anger. But why would I be angry?"

Naomi watched Merriam and Vanessa ready the eggs.

Leslie sighed. "So, you want me to change majors, at this stage—and change it to art, of all things? This is a switch. Most parents stress studying something traditional, more *marketable* to build a career around." She shook her head.

"If I said yes?" Naomi braced for her daughter's response. She turned the bill on her cap to the front and pulled it low, shielding her eyes in shadow. The kitchen noises slackened. Yolanda Adams's "The Battle Is the Lord's" drifted from the CD player. Naomi wanted more activity, more noise. She didn't want their talk overheard.

Leslie turned away, standing with her back to Naomi. "Don't know. But you've got to let me alone on this. Because you asked, I gave in on one thing by commuting to George Mason instead of staying on campus. That should've been enough. Now you want to tell me what to study and how many men I should date."

"I don't stop being your mother because you're in college." Naomi's tone darkened. "And don't tell me what should or shouldn't be enough." She didn't like talking to Leslie's back. Even if they couldn't be overheard, Leslie's back to her surely clued onlookers: their conversation wasn't lovely.

"Theresa asked again if I was interested in rooming with her."

Naomi knew this was coming; it always did. "Meaning?" She understood what Leslie meant, but wanted her to say it.

Leslie shrugged. "I'm just saying."

Naomi tilted the bill on her cap, taking her eyes out of shadow, and retrieved a second tray of potatoes. She then eased around Leslie, facing her. Leaning over the tray she held, she glared at her daughter. "No, you're not 'just saying.' You never 'just say,' and neither do I. I don't like threats, Les; you know that. But if you're sending one? Take the veil off." In her peripheral vision, Naomi noted a few crew members paused in their actions. Heads turned their way; others paused but then continued whatever they were doing. The kitchen smells blended, grew less pungent. Naomi's hunger dissipated.

She wanted her flask.

"Ma, please back off, or I'll take Theresa up on her offer. If not Theresa, then somebody, or I'll get a place of my own." Leslie only met her mother's eyes briefly. Beads of sweat dotted her upper lip.

"You know I want you with me, Leslie."

"*Why*, Ma? Why do you want me with you? Most times, you're busy with your patients and articles. Your life seems full to me. You don't spend your time sitting around the house waiting for me so you can live vicariously through my life. Why is it so important I be with you?"

"I have my reasons." But she didn't. Not anything concrete. Naomi turned away, heading to where Merriam and Vanessa were scrambling eggs. Leslie followed.

It may have been her imagination (Naomi didn't think so), but Merriam and Vanessa became extra busy as she and Leslie approached. "How're we doing over here, ladies?" Naomi rested her potatoes on the counter, and Leslie followed suit.

Merriam whisked the eggs, the muscles in her forearm bulging with each twist of her wrist. "We started these eggs a little early, so we might want to serve sooner instead of waiting. Ben says people have already gravitated our way."

"That okay with you, Naomi?" Vanessa was a mild-mannered woman in her late-30s whose smile could brighten any day. She smiled now.

Naomi smiled back and pulled her Ravens cap back down. "Sure. That's fine. Did Horace's replacement show?"

"Yeah," Merriam answered. "Tammy said he was helping her and Ben set up tables out front. Said he was tall, kinda cute."

"I see. If the eggs are all we're waiting for, and they've got the tables up, we might as well get the line started."

Naomi started away, hoping her daughter would hang back with Vanessa and Merriam.

She was relieved Leslie didn't follow her to meet the new guy. The last thing that girl needed was another man in the mix.

Naomi typically engaged in small talk with the visitors, but this time (to lift her moody blue), she made a detour. Her briefcase was in the back of her silver BMW X5. That's where she headed, soon standing in a wide alleyway outside the cafeteria door.

She'd parked her vehicle perpendicular to the building. It was bright outside; the sun beaming high in the cloudless sky. When she reached her SAV, Naomi paused before opening the cargo area. She didn't give a hey-nonny-nonny about being seen; foremost, she second-guessed taking a drink.

Naomi stood, shifting her weight from one foot to the other, taking her keys out of one pocket, putting them in another. The pull intensified. Her throat clicked, opening and closing with the struggle between anticipation of the familiar and resisting the ill-advised.

Detecting movement, she turned to discover Leslie searching the alley (and decided against retrieving her flask).

She opened the tailgate. Realizing she didn't need it, Naomi removed her Glock-17 semiautomatic from under her shirt and tucked it into the hideaway storage space. She experienced the slightest regret (and irritation) at abandoning her initial impulse, but was proud of herself as she locked her vehicle. She walked toward Leslie, who appeared relieved to see her. "Looking for me?"

Leslie nodded. "We're ready to serve. Ben's got the line forming, but we presumed you'd want to greet Horace's stand-in beforehand, since he's the only new body in the group. He doesn't seem uncomfortable, but it wouldn't hurt."

"Is he as cute as they're saying?"

"If that's your type." Leslie shrugged but adopted a quasi-smile before returning her gaze to Naomi.

If people only knew how often the face and body betrayed the words.
"What type is that?"

"Oh, the typical: tall, dark, and handsome. Light eyes. You know—the usual." Leslie giggled.

"Is that all? Well, let me greet this homely stand-in." She clasped Leslie's forearm, pulling her along.

Naomi stood in the cafeteria doorway, surveying the place for someone fitting Leslie's description. It sounded like he'd be easy to spot, so she didn't stay too long on any one face. The boombox now blasted Dorothy Love Coates and the Gospel Harmonettes singing the uplifting "That's Enough," and Naomi appreciated hearing a poignant dose of old-time female gospel harmony.

She turned to Leslie. "So, where is he?"

Leslie scanned the cafeteria. "He was with Ben and Gary..." Her eyes widened upon seeing him. "Oh, see? There he is."

"Where?"

"Behind the last table. I'd point, but that's impolite."

Naomi concentrated her gaze where Leslie directed and spotted him immediately. She should have spotted him with her initial scan—he wasn't hard to miss. Indeed, he was tall. Given her distance from him, Naomi couldn't discern his light eyes, but even from her vantage point, she could tell he was good-looking.

She continued staring. He seemed familiar to her.

"Ma, that's embarrassing. He's not *that* cute."

"Huh? Oh. No. He looked like a former patient, that's all." It wasn't complete fibnation. For all Naomi knew, he could've been a former patient. But she didn't think so.

Leslie placed hands on her hips, hinting impatience. "Are you greeting the man or not?"

"Can I have a minute first?"

"A minute for what? No, come on." Leslie now gripped Naomi's arm, pulling her along.

Naomi had mixed feelings about meeting him; she stopped short. "That's unnecessary, Les."

"Oh. Sorry."

"Look, let's help serve the food. I can say hello later."

"Why can't you greet 'im now? We're right here."

"I can greet him now. I want to wait. Besides, he's already spoken with a few of you." She glanced the man's way again. "He doesn't seem to be feeling out of place or anything. Let it be."

Leslie shook her head. "Sometimes, I cannot figure you out."

"Then stop trying. Now, let's get this breakfast served." Naomi stepped behind the trays filled with piles of bacon and sausage. Her stomach growled. Staying put, she donned a pair of disposable poly gloves and stood, ready to serve.

Daylight poured through the exit doors and top windows. The overhead lights beamed as well, making the cafeteria unusually bright. The bright room, however, didn't diminish the dimness of the situation. Most of those in the room had no home, likely receiving the only proper meal they'd have for the day.

Naomi never showed pity or excess sympathy (most of their visitors resented it), but a profound sense of loneliness enveloped her when serving them. *I'm only exercising my emotional intelligence here.* She tried avoiding merging her personal and professional worlds, but most times couldn't help it; psychiatrists were rarely off duty.

As people passed through the line, Naomi tried to make eye contact, smile, to say "Hello" (and advised the crew to do the same). It sometimes proved challenging. Most homeless kept their eyes downcast, but some returned the greeting. They had their regulars, of course, who engaged some of the crew in light banter.

A gentle breeze blew through the open exit doors as the crew cleared and cleaned the room. Although accustomed to the low stench of sweat and urine, Naomi was thankful for its noticeable dissipation. Only a few slices of bacon and three sausage links—rooted to their spot by droplets of congealed grease—remained in the tray in front of her. She wasn't hungry anymore (having eaten a few pieces of meat during the serving), but she plucked a slice of bacon and took a bite.

Cold now, the bacon was rubbery; the taste of grease coating portions of the slice muted its smoky flavor. Naomi swallowed against her better judgment, stacked the empty trays, and deliberated the specifics for her next article: "Exploring Attribution Theory."

A man's voice interrupted her thoughts. "Excuse me. Are you Naomi?"

Naomi turned, looking up into the face of the gentleman serving as Horace's replacement. He was attractive—the contrast of his dark-brown skin and hazel eyes arresting. She cleared her throat and extended a hand. "Yes, I'm Naomi. Naomi Alexander." Her hand swam in the depths of the man's palm, but she gripped back.

"I'm Jonathan Rast. Horace Packard's under the weather; asked me to sub for him."

"My apologies for not saying 'hello' sooner, but thank you for coming out. Horace didn't have to send a replacement." Naomi tried not to stare.

Jonathan tilted his head. "Something wrong?" Concern pervaded his direct gaze.

"No. I'm sorry. Anyone in your family involved in the medical field? Doctor, teacher, nurse?"

He shook his head. "I'm in the restaurant business. I own DeTante's downtown. And the rest of the family is involved with that. Why?"

"Well, I'm a therapist. You seem familiar. Thought maybe that was the connection. What about the volunteer stuff?" She realized she sounded like an interrogator, but she needed to know who Jonathan was.

"Let's see... I help with youth literacy; I sometimes volunteer to take pictures for my community newsletter. And, as you can see, I do on-call work." He grinned, revealing a hint of the boy he used to be. "Did that ring any bells? Jog your memory?"

"Not really. But tell you what: it was nice meeting you. Let's finish closing shop. The connection might dawn on me. Do I look familiar?"

"No, ma'am."

"Did you just call me *ma'am?*" She wasn't offended.

"No offense. I'll address all women that way. Younger, older—it doesn't matter."

"Oh, okay. Didn't wanna hafta *hurt* you up in here." Naomi bucked and feigned a punch.

Jonathan chortled with a headshake. "Oh, I'd remember meeting *you* before. Let me know if something comes to you, okay?" He started away, whistling a tune Naomi didn't recognize.

Her smile faded as she watched him go.

She hadn't met Jonathan until today, but she realized why he seemed so familiar. A knot formed in her throat. She coughed several times, attempting to clear it. She hadn't met him before but had a hunch about him—experienced a flash of truth—one not favorable.

It told her plainly: the man wouldn't live much longer. She couldn't conjure auras at will but believed faint and fading hues of any color would emanate from him if she could.

Naomi didn't consider herself psychic by any stretch of the imagination. She knew no specifics of his death (no date, time, place, or manner), only the certainty of its imminence. This flash of truth carried dread for a man she didn't know.

She wondered why she didn't get a similar hunch the day she watched her husband leave for doughnuts.

Naomi resumed assisting with the cleanup. She chatted here and there with a few of the homeless, who, having no next place to go, hung around the cafeteria after breakfast ended. Done with the cleanup, she said her goodbyes, levels of moody blue reclaiming her.

Her goodbye to Jonathan was pleasant but curt.

She hoped to see him again, maybe visit his restaurant.

It was her stab at denial.

LSB: Pause Button

No, S.F.! Don't pause the story now! Say it ain't so!

- What happens, with Rick & Viv's relationship?

- How does Rick deal with Viv, Jonathan, the underlying issue with Louise, and therapy with Naomi?

- What in the world does Naomi have to do with all of this, given that 'aura-flicker' and 'flash-of-truth' about Jonathan? And what's behind that strange vibe she has with her daughter, Leslie?

Your interest pleases me!

The answers to these questions (plus other good stuff arising as the story unfolds) await you inside the tale, found in both digital and bound formats at book retailers online!

Get *Like Sweet Buttermilk*:

I'll see you after "The End." Happy reading!

Up next: a preview of book 2, *Obscure Boundaries*...

Obscure Boundaries

Book 2

Prologue

Months Ago

"*L*imitations bind you," the Voice stated with soft, modulated sound, ringing with crystal-clear intonation.
"It's okay. Our love sustains him," she answered.
Silence.
"I don't want to scare him."
"You may, but your love secures him," the Voice answered.
"And my others?"
"As I know, so do you."
"...It's not much time."
"It will be enough."

Chapter 1

Rocks and Hard Places

H e was hot and bothered, and it had nothing to do with the outdoor temperature.

In fact, it was cool for early September.

Jeff Winthrop sat back in his Adirondack chair of stained-ipe, running a palm over his bald head. He shifted his hips right and left, trying to contain a heated drive edging closer to an uncompromising desire entirely new to him. He wanted, in point-blank succinctness, to make love to his wife.

And therein lay the problem.

He wanted his wife. But she was dead. Had been for over three years. Besides that, he'd remarried, so his *wife* piddled around somewhere inside the house. But she was not whom he wanted.

He wanted *Julia*.

Jeff ran a palm over his head again; his body presented an obvious clue to his state of mind. Good thing he was alone.

"Jeffy?" Ruth's voice trailed through the window from the kitchen area, a sound both grating and lilting.

He cringed, rolling his eyes upward with an annoyed sigh he kept at whisper level. He hated being called that. *Hated it.* With a passion. He was 48 years old: damn-near 50. His mama never called him that; why did she insist on doing it?

Irritated, he didn't answer. Let her come searching for him (not that he looked forward to her finding him).

Ruth's interruption, however, didn't affect the hardness in his pants. He heard Ruth move to the kitchen bay window, felt her looking out at him. He didn't move. Instead, he focused on the treetops above the view of the alley and neighboring homes.

He loved living on Capitol Hill in Washington, DC. Loved the ethnic mix of its residents and the varying architectural styles of its homes. DC was a hub of diversity: lifestyle, socializing, art, politics, and culture. Ruth hinted many times about moving to the suburbs of Montgomery County, Maryland, but Jeff wasn't interested.

It was a mistake.

Maybe it was, perhaps it wasn't. Didn't matter now, anyway. He'd married her. What's done is done. Rome wasn't built in a day. No use crying over spilled milk. He was in it to win it. Apply other platitudes as needed.

Jeff concentrated on the trees (the leaves would change soon), willing his erection to subside while he was still alone. He didn't sense Ruth watching him anymore. He figured she'd be joining him any minute.

A balmy breeze interrupted the cool, still Saturday morning. Strangely, the light wind somehow carried the timeless scent of Guerlain's Shalimar. An infusion of bergamot, iris, vanilla, jasmine, and roses filled Jeff's nostrils and dissipated in an instant, as if Julia sprinted past him.

His penis throbbed with newfound intensity. Jeff whispered, "Shit," and shifted his hips again. He needed to get it together.

Several houses down, the Stewart family's Rottweiler, Genesis, barked. Jeff turned his attention in the direction Genesis sounded his notification: toward the alley's entrance farthest away. His daughter, Mallory, slowed to a trot, finishing her morning run.

She waved as she approached their backyard.

He waved back.

A shuffling noise came through the bay window. The refrigerator door opened and then closed. It was too early for his son, Todd, to be out of bed, so it had to be Ruth continuing to make her presence known. But she stayed inside, and Jeff wondered if she'd changed her mind about joining him on the deck.

Mallory released the latch on the six-foot split-board fence and entered their yard with a wide smile. "Hi, Daddy."

"Mornin', M-Sweet." Jeff smiled back at his daughter, but knowing Ruth was nearby, his smile faltered with a mixture of pride...and mild irritation.

Since he'd married Ruth, Mallory hadn't been the least bit cooperative. She displayed abject tolerance—no more, no less. Since he never discussed Mallory's concerns with her in depth, some of the blame was his, but he didn't want to give the impression he needed his daughter's approval regarding decisions he made for his family.

Mallory's attitude toward Ruth aside, Jeff was proud of his daughter. At 16, she'd pursued and accomplished much academically, such that she could have skipped her junior year to be a senior at her private high school. He admired her decision to stay in her correct grade, and her work with underprivileged kids through the museum-sponsored art program also struck a chord with him. Mallory reminded him of Julia a lot—even though anyone could see he spit her out.

She crossed their concrete patio and started up the wooden steps leading to their deck.

Erection still hanging around, but at half-mast now, Jeff tugged his shirttail down as best he could, then slid the newspaper from the table, placing it in his lap for additional cover.

Mallory eyed the scenery while guzzling from the water bottle she left on the top step. Sweat beaded her brow and upper lip, lines of sweat trickled from her temples. Her plum-colored running gear (water-wicking tank and shorts) was only damp in spots. Finished drinking, she cocked her head and cut her eyes his way. "What's wrong, Daddy?"

"Nothing. Why?"

"Daddy..."

"Did you have a good run?"

She shrugged. "I guess. I always like it better when I head away from the Capitol." She used her forearm to clear the sweat from her face. "You didn't answer my question. What's wrong?"

"I did answer you. You going to see Todd play today?" His erection now subsided, Jeff put the newspaper back on the table.

Mallory sprung a half-smile. "These scrimmages don't even count, but yeah, Kelz and I will be there to cheer him on." She chugged more of her water.

Jeff tried to maintain a neutral expression but obviously failed.

"What now? Elliot?" With a shake of her head, Mallory twisted her lips and shifted her gaze away from him. "I've told you over and over. We're friends, Daddy. *Friends.* That's it."

"I know what you've told me. And I believe *you* see him as just a friend. But I have my doubts about that going both ways. Does Elliot have a girlfriend?"

"Not anymore, no."

"And he's not gay?" He didn't have a problem with Mallory having a boyfriend. And if the young man was gay, that was fine, too. He actually liked "Kelz." Elliot was clean-cut, respectful. But Jeff believed his role as her father was reinforcing the perception he was a hard sell for the males (or females if so ordered) in her life, regardless of whom M-Sweet brought into their home.

An odd expression crossed Mallory's face. "God, no."

"And you're so sure of this because...?"

She smirked at him. "Trust me, not for any of the reasons you're thinking. Look, Daddy, Kelz is cool people, and I get along better with him than with most of my so-called girlfriends." Her smirk shifted to a soft smile. "See, you're used to best friends being gender respective. These days, you're just friends with who you're friends with. It doesn't matter what sex they are—or what sexual orientation. But again, Elliot is not gay. And even if he was," Mallory shrugged, "I'd still be good friends with him."

"Listen to you, 'gender respective.' That private school has you ready to skip senior year next year and go right on to college."

"Uh, not quite, Daddy." She leaned against the railing behind her and folded her arms. "Are you going to tell me what's wrong?"

"I already did."

"C'mon; I know you."

And she did. He had a strong father-daughter bond with M-Sweet, laced with good friendship vibes, but Jeff couldn't let his daughter in on this one. His horniness for her mother wasn't father-daughter material. An image of Julia's electrocardiogram flatlining surfaced in his mind in tandem with the most profound urge to weep. "I'm fine, M-Sweet. You eatin' somethin'?" He wanted nothing more than to be alone.

"I don't know, I guess."

The sound of cookware being placed on the stove came through the window, accompanied by Ruth's humming. Jeff didn't know the tune—most likely something gospel. He and Mallory exchanged a look holding at least two years' worth of lost conversation, reminding him of one plain truth: he'd messed up. Jeff reached inward for another platitude, determined to make figurative lemonade from life's lemons.

Leaning back with interlocked fingers supporting his head, Jeff spoke first. "I think you should eat, but it's up to you."

Mallory shifted her gaze to the window but said nothing. After some seconds, she shook her head.

"What?" Jeff smiled, wanting to ease the tension brewing underneath such a tolerant atmosphere.

M-Sweet turned to him but didn't smile back. She held her water bottle poised at her mouth. "Nothing, Daddy." She drained the bottle.

As much as he loved his daughter, he didn't feel like probing to find out what was wrong with her (not this morning, anyway). He held his tongue.

The left panel of their french doors opened, and Ruth stepped onto the deck. Jeff read the slightest hint of irritation on her face before she smiled wide with merriment, her green eyes shining. "Morning meeting? What'd I miss?"

Ignoring Ruth's initial expression, he smiled back. "Not a thing. Just seeing if Mal was going to Todd's scrimmage, which she is."

Ruth turned her eyes to Mallory. "Oh, good. At least your dad will have some company." The smile she sent her stepdaughter wavered in its merriment.

"Uh-huh." Mallory offered a perfunctory upturn of her lips and then focused on the backs of the houses across the alley. His daughter was quite mature regarding her schoolwork and work-study activities, even her friends. But when it came to Ruth, Mallory acted every bit the 16-year-old teenager she was.

He caught Ruth's glance at him: a glance telling him she wanted him to say something in her defense about Mallory's response.

Jeff wanted to say something all right, but nothing his present audience would like to hear. He wanted to tell them both to get their shit together and leave him out of it. He'd married Ruth; no intention of divorcing her, so she wasn't going anywhere. Mallory needed to get over it. Mallory was his daughter, his blood; she sure as hell wasn't going anywhere. Ruth needed to swallow that pill and get over it.

Jeff sighed (a deep rumble in his throat). He shifted his gaze back and forth between the women. Ruth and Mallory looked at him expectantly, each wearing expressions of self-satisfaction as if they'd each won some unvoiced challenge, of which Jeff's siding was the prize.

Nothing out on this deck but rocks and hard places.

He shifted focus toward the alley. Genesis barked again as a Buick Century entered the alleyway. Jeff stretched his long legs out between them, the extension serving as an unintended line of division.

He studied the tops of his New Balance running shoes, thinking he should have run this morning himself. If he had, the likelihood of being on the deck in this situation would have been diminished. But he didn't run this morning, so here he was.

Without looking up (and resisting the impulse and desire to get up, go into the house, and leave them on the deck), Jeff again assumed the role of mediator. "Look, for a change, why don't we *all* try to be there?" He spoke to Ruth: "Todd's scrimmage isn't until three. Why don't you stop by the field during a break between one of your showings?"

Ruth's stiff smile signaled his response wasn't satisfactory. "I'll see."

His daughter mumbled something indistinct.

He turned his attention to her. "You were saying, Mallory?"

Mallory offered the same stiff smile. "Nothing."

Ruth sighed. "See, Jeff? I'm trying. But we will not get anywh—" She stopped short. "You need to talk to her, Jeff—with some firm direction this time. She needs to attend church more, too. A good sermon won't hurt her. It seems she's forgotten about honoring thy mother and father."

Jeff kept his eyes on his daughter, knowing what was coming.

Mallory, at first leaning against the deck railing, stood straight. She pointed her water bottle at Ruth before holding it down at her side. "First, I'm standing right here, so stop talking about me as if I weren't. Second, I honor my father—and my mother: my mother's *memory*. *You* are not my mother." Her brown eyes were wide, filled with anger, but also traces of what appeared to be wary trepidation.

Jeff stood. His suggestion that they all watch Todd play was middle-of-the-road, what seemed an ideal compromise. And still, neither was happy. He knew deeper issues swirled around them, unseen and unspoken, out there on the deck with them, but he didn't have whatever he needed to deal with it right now (or ever?). "Stop it, both of you."

The scent of Shalimar wafted past him again. Jeff narrowed his focus on Ruth and then Mallory, seeing if either detected it. Neither showed any sign of noticing a change in the aromatic atmosphere, but Mallory jerked her head around as if startled. Did she smell it, too, then? He leaned toward his daughter but froze, hesitant to ask her: the notion was just too crazy. Wasn't it?

Time stood still as Julia's scent faded. Damn, he wanted her.

"Jeffy?" Ruth prompted in a soft voice.

Jeff shifted his gaze to her, clenching his teeth against the awful sound of that nickname in his ears. It was still summer, but she stood before him in a lightweight fleece sweat suit of azure-blue, matching Adidas footwear, her freshly permed, ash-brown hair tied back in a ponytail. Zeta-Phi-Beta earrings dangled, announcing her affiliation. And although she'd be changing into business attire in a few hours, she was dressed and ready to go at seven twenty-seven on a lazy Saturday morning. But that was Ruth; she preferred being ready to pick up and go. Unlike Julia, Ruth cared little for lounging in sweats and a T-shirt.

He could list a slew of *unlike-Julia* instances, but that was counter-productive to making the best of how he had to live his life now.

Ruth stepped closer, looking up at him. At five feet eight inches, she'd need another five inches to be as tall as him. She studied his face.

Jeff studied hers.

Her moisturized buttercream skin glowed. He liked her better without makeup, and she wore none now. Her hair pulled back from her face, however, accentuated her broad, slightly bulbous forehead, which gleamed like a beacon as he watched her. The size of her forehead didn't detract from her overall attractiveness. So, for those who liked her type, oh yeah, Ruth was as fine as she wanted to be (if you liked that type).

But when it came down to it, Jeff didn't prefer her type. He liked them shorter, browner, small-breasted, and round-assed. He liked the springy, textured feel of the naturally coiled roots of a Black woman's clean and unprocessed hair, twisted or locked and styled in so many alluring ways. Thus, his "type" nosedived in contrast to the physical features of his second wife—and dovetailed with the features of his first.

He did like Ruth, though.

Mallory leaned forward, peering up into his face. "Daddy?"

Jeff smiled at her. He wanted to get whatever was going on in this moment over with. They'd be into it again sometime later, anyway. "Come on, guys." He shook his head, maintaining the smile. "I'm not trying to do this right now. I want to see my boy play; that's it." He alternated gazes at both women before sitting again. He lost the smile.

Mallory leaned back against the railing. "That's all I want to do, too."

Jeff nodded at her. "Thanks, M-Sweet." He shifted attention to Ruth.

Her green eyes, a shade blending pear and olive (although his daughter deemed them "crocodile-green"), showed a shade paler, but she didn't speak. With Ruth, her irises seeming to wash out wasn't a good thing.

Mallory slid between the railing and his chair. Standing behind him, she planted a kiss atop his head. "I've said all I wanted to say, and I think I'll pass on breakfast."

He tilted his head back, peering at Mallory upside down. "You sure?"

She grinned. "Yeah." She kissed his forehead and went into the house without looking Ruth's way.

One down, one to go.

Jeff sat upright, staring past Ruth and down the alley, bracing himself for her reaction. She rarely let anything go; there was always some...blowback.

Ruth moved between his legs and kneeled, resting her forearms on his thighs. She sighed yet again.

He forced his gaze in her general direction.

"It's been over two years, Jeff, and things aren't much better." Her voice shook but carried more attitude than wistful observation.

"She needs time." *We all do*, he wanted to add.

"And Todd?"

"What about him?"

"Does he need time, too?"

"I don't know. But it's different with boys."

She crooked one corner of her mouth. "Yeah, okay."

Jeff now locked his eyes on hers, thinking (just maybe) Mallory's assessment of Ruth's eye color was truer than not—with a significance beyond their shade. Crocodiles. "What, Ruth?"

She sighed long and hard while looking skyward, then closed her eyes. "'Many are the afflictions of the righteous: but the Lord delivereth him out of them all.'" She returned her gaze to Jeff. "Psalms: chapter thirty-four, verse nineteen." She offered a small smile.

Now it was his turn to smirk. "Yeah, okay." He looked away, doing his best to keep his emotions in check. He knew she meant well, but...

They grew quiet. She squeezed his thigh. Any more pressure and her grip would have hurt. "And what about you, Jeffrey Adair Winthrop, the third? Do you need more time?"

Her grip, more than her words, captured his attention. He aligned his gaze with hers. "No, I don't, Ruth L. Cannon-Winthrop." Oh, but he did; he truly did. He needed all kinds of time.

Her grip on his thigh slackened as she held his gaze. Finally, she stood. "You know, Jeff, the kids take their cue from you. Think about that."

Jeff didn't respond. Even if her words were legit, he wasn't thinking about anything. He just wanted her to go.

"Why the fuck did you marry me, Jeff?"

Shaking his head, he let out a low breath. Bible quotes one minute, blue language the next. Nevertheless, she posed a valid question. He'd need even more time to ponder a valid answer.

"Never mind, Jeff." She stood with a huff, but after some seconds, drifted to stand behind him.

Never mind was right. He couldn't do the verbal give-and-take with her this morning—not with reminders of Julia swirling around him. But he couldn't allow his mood to mess with the rest of Ruth's Saturday, either. Jeff tilted his head back to her. "It'll be fine."

He could tell his response wasn't what she wanted or expected, but Ruth nodded anyway. She rested a palm on his forehead, then ran it back across his scalp. "You know what? I'm looking forward to seeing this doctor of yours next week. What's her name again?"

He stared past her, up at the slow-moving clouds. "Naomi. Doctor Naomi Alexander."

"Yeah, that's it. Maybe she can help. Todd being on the roof like that was concerning. You three may have cut your grief counseling with her too soon."

He contained a scoff. She didn't have the slightest idea what she was talking about. Or maybe she did. Jeff focused on the clouds, images of his son sitting on the roof in the rain two nights ago intruding. Even through that rain drenching his face, Todd's eyes had been so—

Ruth ran her hand over his head again, adding caresses to the back of his neck. She shifted some, leaning forward enough to block his line of vision with the clouds, in essence forcing him to look at her. To look away or avert his gaze would have sent a rudely unmistakable message or implied a victory of sorts for Ruth he had no intention of giving. He held her gaze.

A smile snaked her lips. "Winter's coming. It'll be getting cold out. Think you might let your hair grow this season? For me?"

Here she goes with this mess again. "Ruth..."

"I just want to see what you look like with hair."

"You've seen pictures."

"That's not the same thing, and you know it." She paused, her hand resting on his head. "Come on. At least some facial hair. Please?"

"We'll see," Jeff said, knowing full well they wouldn't see. Besides, he'd taken Julia's pictures down. Every single one. The kids had pictures of her in their rooms (he stood firm on that), but otherwise... So, as far as he was concerned, Ruth had reached her limit for "please me" concessions. He sat up, welcoming the disconnection from her caress. He checked his watch for no other reason than to give the semblance of caring about the time. "I think I'll skip breakfast, too. Make a run." Run where? He didn't know. But that wasn't the point. "See you at the scrimmage later?" He casually scanned the surrounding area—everywhere but back at her. Her response would tell him all he needed to know. Still, he didn't want her to touch him again.

"I won't be able to stay for the whole thing," she confided in a tone low but affable. She didn't touch him.

Jeff nodded, knowing as much already. "Going anywhere right now?"

"Not for a couple hours. Why?"

"No reason. Just make sure Todd puts something in his stomach." He had yet to look at her.

"Sure."

At last, he turned to his wife.

She smiled at him. "So, we're good?"

Jeff reached for the front of Ruth's sweat jacket. He drew her down and pecked her lips. "We're fine."

A hand on her hip, Ruth viewed the alleyway and blew a breath. "No one's eating but me. Guess I'll have a muffin and scrambled egg."

"Sounds good." What did she want him to say? What *could* he say?

"Okay, well...," she trailed off.

He hated awkward silences. "Go 'head, Ruth. I'll see you at the game. Maybe we'll talk more later. But give me a minute, okay?"

She patted his shoulder before retreating into the house. And, as light and fleeting as that pat was, it still annoyed him.

Jeff scanned the yards and backs of houses in the alley, seeing them but not really. He wanted that scent, Julia's scent, to waft past him again. He wanted that more than anything. Jeff waited a few minutes, hoping for it.

He drew a palm over his scalp. Ruth's request that he let his hair grow irked him.

He'd shaved his hair after losing a bet to Julia over college football. She loved him bald, so he never allowed his hair to grow back. On the first anniversary of Julia's death, he shaved his facial hair and didn't allow that to grow back, either. The act, for him, demonstrated symbolic homage to her. Jeff sometimes missed having hair, but he'd also grown used to not having it. He didn't know if he was going bald for real. Perhaps a derivative of his trace Native American ancestry negated any hair-loss genes in his African American gene pool; he'd never seen a balding Indigenous. His uncles had heads full of hair, and the youngest was 62. So, whatever the DNA case, there was hope. Ruth's request aside, every so often, even he was curious about how he'd look with hair now.

But Julia likes him bald, so…

Jeff cut his eyes to the hammock and other deck furniture stacked on the opposite side of the deck. He figured his chore for today would be to move it all to the storage shed on the patio below.

Six years ago, he and Julia brought the hammock back from a trip to Cancun, Mexico. He'd been in it once, maybe twice, since she died (always alone, never with Ruth). The hammock held a delightful assortment of happy, warm, and erotic memories, such that the idea of getting rid of it violated something sacrosanct. Yet the idea of getting back in it to reconnect with Julia seemed an inherent imperative. Jeff's thoughts shifted to a warm night four summers ago. His groin stirred again with memories of what they were up to in that hammock.

He shook his head, sending his gaze upward. "I'm fucked," he whispered to the clouds. If the bright, blue sky and pearly-white clouds were any indication, the day would be perfect for football—and they seemed to agree (wispily) with the whispered status of his predicament.

Wanting to wait, but knowing it was stupid to wait for Julia's scent to return, Jeff inspected the deck furniture. Admittedly, Julia warned against purchasing the cast-iron ensemble. *"That is going to bleed rust right onto the wood,"* she'd commented.

Jeff stooped for closer inspection of the meranti wood upon which the cast-iron chairs and table rested. He traced fingers across some of the rust stains, smiling to himself.

Before she died, Julia was head RN at Washington Hospital Center. But her medical knowledge contributed only a tiny part of her entire knowledge base. Julia knew a little or a lot about all kinds of stuff: the relationship between Mother Nature and home improvements being no exception. Jeff's small smile morphed into mild confusion as he tried to remember why he'd gotten the furniture anyway.

An infusion of iris, vanilla, and roses wafted across his nose again.

He shot to his feet, examining the surrounding area with squinted focus.

Genesis barked fiercely, but no one and no thing appeared out of place. The serene atmosphere, however, prickled the nonexistent hair on his scalp.

Jeff took hesitant seconds lowering back into his Adirondack chair.

What is going on?

He slowly shook his head, his eyes searching the deck and alley for something deemed impossible to see—something his nose told him...was right before his eyes.

Their appointment with Dr. Alexander was scheduled for later in the coming week.

But if this shit keeps up...

Jeff realized he'd need an emergency private session with her much sooner.

Chapter 2

Doughnut Dreams

"*I*'m off to Dunkin' Donuts. Who wants what?" *Tyson says. He fixes his walnut-brown eyes on Naomi and smiles.*

Naomi feels a vestige of something not quite nameable inside but smiles back at her husband. "I want you to help me finish getting these begonias planted; that's what I want. But I'll take a half-dozen maple-iced, thanks, since my needs and wants are quite interchangeable at the moment."

"Uh-huh," Tyson replies. He turns to Leslie. "What do you have a taste for, Punkin?"

Naomi turns to Leslie, too.

Leslie removes her gardening gloves and swipes a wrist over her sweaty (and sparsely muddy) brow. "Uh, I don't know: two powdered raspberry jellies, two glazed apple-filled, and two powdered lemon-filled, I guess."

"You 'guess'?" Tyson's thin mustache twitches as his lips curl into a sardonic grin. His sardonic grin always gives Naomi a secret tingle.

Naomi gazes at her daughter, wondering when she put her forehead in the dirt.

Leslie grins back at her father. The childish expression contrasts sharply but approvingly with the young-adult maturity claiming her features. She is 16, looking more in her 20s. Or is she in her 20s, looking all of 16?

Watching the exchange between father and daughter, Naomi feels the unnamable tinge again. "Leslie, bring me another bag of soil from the garage, would you please?"

"Sure, Ma." Leslie shoots another smile at her father. "Bye, Daddy." There is something very final about how she says, *Bye, Daddy.* She retreats backward toward their opened garage, located several feet behind everyone.

"Well, is it like *that*? 'Bye, Daddy'? I'm just going to get doughnuts." Tyson faces Leslie as he speaks, so his back is to Naomi.

Leslie smiles again but doesn't look at her father. Instead, she locks eyes with her mother, and the unnamable inkling defines itself: foreboding. It seems hours pass before Naomi tears her gaze from Leslie's. "Tyson, don't go."

Tyson shifts his attention to her, keenly handsome in his Philadelphia Eagles cap. His mustache twitches again, but he doesn't smile this time. His expression is somber yet knowing. "You know I have to," he whispers.

The unsettling foreboding soon commingles with the ache of sorrow.

"Bye, Daddy." This time, the finality in Leslie's parting words rings clear.

"I love you, Punkin. Raspberry, apple-filled, and lemon-filled, right?"

Leslie nods, her face on the verge of teary crumple.

Tyson turns to Naomi. "Maple-iced for you." He paused, his brown eyes reflecting a gracious regret. "And you will love again."

Heartbroken, Naomi fights her tears. "I don't want to."

"Thank you. But I can't do anything with that." The cute sardonic grin returns. Tyson shrugs and heads for his Toyota Avalon.

"...Don't go, Danny Boy." But these words never cross her lips, remaining lodged in her sorrow-choked throat.

Nightfall.

From the sofa in her living room, Naomi stares at a Dunkin' Donuts box resting on the island counter in the kitchen. A reading lamp glows in the corner of the living room. No lights are on in the kitchen, but Naomi sees every detail of what she knows to be a half-empty Dunkin' Donuts box on the counter. Even the emerald-green granite countertop emits a soft glow, as if the box of doughnuts displayed in a jeweler's glass case and a spotlight shone down on it. Half-empty or filled beyond capacity, the box of sweet treats represents utter aberration given the context of...everything else. Music comes from the stereo, but Naomi doesn't hear it—she just knows it's on.

"Uh-hem," Tyson says, clearing his throat. He sits in a leather recliner in the same corner as the reading lamp. A hardback book rests in his lap. Naomi can't tell what holds his attention but is pretty sure it is a non-fiction work (a biography, most probable).

Tyson looks up from his book and smiles at Naomi. Something about how his glasses have come partway down his nose appeals to her.

"Why are you way over there looking all cute?" Naomi asks her husband. She can hear music playing now—but not quite.

"Well, where should I be?" The melodic timbre of Tyson's voice is arousing (and slightly out of place for him).

Naomi pats the space on the sofa next to her. No, the Dunkin' Donuts box shouldn't be there, and no, Tyson shouldn't be, either, but Naomi grabs for the happiness, nonetheless. She raises an eyebrow. "Right here would be a good place to start."

Tyson shakes his head slowly and thumbs toward the stairs. His nostrils flare the tiniest bit with the suggestion. Tyson shifts his hips in his seat, and Naomi knows his erection is stiffening.

She shakes her head and pats the space next to her again, then rises and glides over to Tyson. Kneeling between his legs, she takes his book from him. "I didn't think you'd come back to me," she whispers.

"I know." Tyson pulls Naomi close and kisses her.

Closing her eyes in acceptance and delight, she returns his kiss, but the faint sensation of him equates to rendering him near nonexistent. Naomi opens her eyes: Tyson is still there.

There is a switch in location, or time, maybe both (doughnut dreams were unpredictable), and Naomi realizes she and Tyson are in bed, their bed, together. He feels good (nothing new), and there is music (but not, not quite). Another shift (different bedding, different bed). Naomi and Tyson lie on their sides, facing each other as mutual exploration ensues. Naomi's fingertips explore the contours of her husband's back while Tyson's lips explore the hollow spot above her collarbone. Tyson pulls her closer for a deep kiss, moving his hands soothingly down her back to squeeze and caress her backside.

Tyson isn't (wasn't?) a smoker, but a hint of menthol lingers on his tongue and at the back of his throat. The taste is strange and wonderful in the darkness of their bedroom, and Naomi wants more. As if sensing the change in her desire, Tyson's hands caress the sensitive spot between her shoulder blades. A sigh escapes her lips but breaks as her breath halts somewhere around her tonsils.

Something cold and unyielding slinks into Naomi's center.

The caress continues at her upper back, but Naomi realizes Tyson's hands are still at her backside. Fear and understanding of that implication move through her with icy-cruel certainty as she allows Tyson to take their kiss even deeper. She can't help shivering from a new sense of foreboding—there were too many hands.

Fingertips at Naomi's back glide to her shoulders, and she freezes. Strains of melody tease her ears. Not wanting to leave Tyson (this time with him was always special) but desperately wanting to resist responding to the knowing strokes at her shoulders and back, Naomi concentrates on the faint strains of music playing (but not, *not quite*).

Her husband shifts his left hand to the front of her thigh, sending it upward. An unmistakable rigidness jabs her there, too. She has missed him and wants this to go on forever. But the music is louder now, which is good, because Naomi can also feel herself responding to the other caress from behind her—and that is not good.

She concentrates harder on the music, wanting the escape into the familiar. The hand on her shoulder travels over and down toward the soft swell of her right breast. Naomi forces deeper concentration on the music because she can feel herself disengaging from Tyson's kiss for a glimpse at the owner of the other hands, and she doesn't want to do that.

Besides, she knows who it is.

This understanding mobilizes the fear. Concentration brings clarity to the music, but *Naomi's head is still turning away from Tyson to the other. Violins play as the familiarity of the music imparts the desired escape—but it comes seconds too late. Naomi sees the face: Leslie.*

Naomi bolted upright in her bed, simultaneously striking the snooze button on her alarm clock and instantly silencing Beethoven's Violin Sonata No. 5 in F major, Op. 24, *Spring*. She took several deep, calming breaths, sending unwelcomed remnants of her sleeping session away. As disturbing as the dream was, perspiration didn't dampen her body. She'd had one of the few variations of oft-recurring dreams about Tyson. This was the first to include Leslie in such a way, but Naomi hesitated to call this latest a nightmare.

Naomi swung her legs over the side of her bed. She struck the alarm clock a second time to allow Beethoven to float into the bedroom again, but *Spring* had ended. Chopin's The Prelude in E minor No. 4, Op. 28 filled the surrounding space instead.

She reached under her pillow and grasped her Glock-17 semi-automatic pistol. After checking the safety, she placed the gun back in its holster before tossing it onto the leather satchel resting in her reading chair.

Dr. Naomi Alexander padded to her bathroom to start her day. It was six forty-five a.m. A combined total of three and a half hours sleep (albeit broken): her most extended sleep session in months.

Not bad.

Chapter 3

Generation "Why?"

"I just know, I'm not sayin' jack." Mallory Èkerie Winthrop held the phone's receiver to her ear with her shoulder as she dug into her backpack for yet another piece of chewing gum.

She maintained a ten-to-fifteen-stick-a-day habit now that she was trying to quit biting her fingernails. Three years of biting her nails resulted in them having such a nasty, ugly look—never mind the tenderness and occasional trickles of blood from times her stress had her biting past the pain (or maybe even for the pain). Her nails were growing nicely with her switch to gum-chewing; that was encouraging. The switch from fingernails to gum originated from a passing suggestion from Dr. Alexander when they first started going to her (before her dad cut things short), a recommendation Mallory jotted down in her journal, forgot about, and then later came across and decided to try. She didn't know where that journal was now.

"How're you going to attend therapy with your family and say nothing?" Elliot "Kelz" Kelton sounded preoccupied at his end of the phone. More than a classmate, he was one of her best friends. Kelz was comical but a good listener, too.

Mallory reclined against her headboard. She gazed around her bedroom, deciding how to redecorate it. "I'm not going with my 'family,' as you put it."

"Mister Winthrop and Todd are your family, Mal."

"That's right. *My dad and brother.* Not her."

"I got what you were saying the first time. Still, it doesn't look like she's going anywhere, anytime soon, so..."

"Look, call me back on my cell. I don't want to talk about this on the house phone." She didn't want to talk about it at all.

"Oh, right. I forgot. Hold on."

A few seconds later, her cellphone emitted hip-hop music. She viewed her phone's LCD: Elliot. Mallory tapped her cellphone to accept his call and disconnected from the cordless house phone. "Uh-huh."

"Yeah. I was saying the lady isn't going anywhere, so you need to figure something out. How long has she been with you guys?"

"Around two years, give or take some months. Why?"

"And how long your mom's been gone?"

Mallory knew he meant no harm, but his question still hurt. "Three years ago, this past June. Your point?"

"Nothing. I'm just saying. As much as you talk about how your parents loved each other, it didn't take long for your dad to hook up again."

"Don't go there, Kelz." She wasn't going to let Elliot tarnish the memory of her parents' relationship—even if she did have questions about that herself.

Elliot changed the subject. "You work tomorrow, don't you?"

Mallory changed it right back. "She constantly voices these subtle digs at my mother, trying to insult her memory and whatnot when my mother hasn't done a thing to her. And I don't like how she treats Todd."

"I thought you didn't want to go there. And Todd can handle himself; he's almost fifteen."

"I said leave my parents' relationship alone. I have plenty to say about Ruth; you know that. And Todd..." Kelz didn't know about Todd sitting on the roof in the rain (hugging his knees and rocking), and she hadn't been able to talk to her brother about that yet herself.

"'And Todd,' what?"

Mallory reached for another stick of gum. "Todd's not an assertive person. He's mostly shy, given his asthma, and still dealing with Mommy being gone. But I think Ruth started in on him from the beginning. She's had some time to break him down."

"Man, you've got a case of Wicked Stepmother Syndrome bad." He scoffed in friendship.

"Whatever, Kelz." She sucked her teeth. "I don't understand why he married her. I mean, *why?* Why did he do that?"

"It's a generational thing, I guess. Your dad's a baby-boomer, X-er?"

"Not sure. 'X-er,' I think. These titles for the different generations are too much: Boomers, Gen-X, Gen-Y, millennials, Gen-Z, Centennials..." She sucked her teeth.

Kelz snickered. "Right now, you sound more like generation 'Why?'—the question, not the letter."

Mallory formed a halfhearted smile at that comment. "Anyway, I'm not feeling her. Never have. There's something about her. But Daddy..." Mallory trailed off with a wince, reflecting on the talk her father had with Todd and her about Ruth being in his life; this, after Mallory noticed him mentioning Ruth more and more. It wasn't much of a talk, not really an exchange of points of view. Daddy said Ruth was joining the family. And so, she did. Mallory paused before adding: "Besides, he didn't have to get rid of the condo, anyway."

"You said Ruth ended up getting your family much money for that, even if you don't need it."

"True." Nobody said Ruth wasn't a good realtor; Mallory just didn't think Ruth was good for her dad—or their family, period.

"Your dad hold on to the property in Warfield, Virginia?"

"Yeah. He only got rid of the condo because it had too many memories tied to Mommy. The condo used to be their little getaway spot. I think he wanted to rent it out and leave it to us, but Ruth convinced him she could get him a nice piece of change for it because the market was right or whatever." And now that Mallory thought about it, maybe Ruth was on a mission to get rid of memories of Mommy as early as then. She made him take her pictures down. It was possible. Made sense.

"So, Ruth increased both your trust funds, then."

"Everything is not about the dollar. If he hadn't wanted to explore options for the property, he never would have met her."

"Yeah, but it woulda been some other realtor."

"Whatever. It wouldn't have been her."

"Damn!"

"What?" She shook her head, fighting tears. "Never mind; you don't understand."

"Your dad exhibiting some of his stuff this year? It's been a while."

"A piece or two, maybe, but on the real, I doubt it. Daddy's not into his art like he used to be." He wasn't into much of anything like he used to be, except—

"Since your mom's...?"

"Uh-huh." Mallory tried her best not to cry. She missed her mother. And (being honest) she missed her dad, too.

A peculiar knock sounded at her door—two slow knocks followed by two rapid ones: Todd.

"Hold on, Kelz." Mallory held her cellphone away from her mouth, directing her voice toward her bedroom door. "Come in, big head."

Todd Audric Winthrop opened Mallory's door a crack. She could only see one eye as he peered in at her. She missed her mother and wanted her dad back, but she had her brother. That bond made the rest bearable. With Ruth in their lives, though, Todd grew more and more withdrawn.

Mallory frowned at him. "What're you doing?"

"My head's so big; this is all I can fit through the door."

She held in a chuckle. "Oh, li'l brother's got jokes—the *unfunny* kind. What d'you want?"

Todd kept peering with one eye. "Nothin'. Trying to figure out what to eat. Want half a Dagwood?" The door and frame muffled his voice.

"Yeah, but don't make the super. Where's Daddy?"

Her brother opened the door wider for her, showing his entire face. His expression spoke volumes.

Mallory spoke into the phone: "Kelz, you want to hold a minute, or want me to call you back? ...Okay, 'bout half an hour? A'ight." Mallory disconnected with a phone tap and turned back to her brother. She sat forward, whispering, *"Again?"* She shook her head in disbelief, but a more significant part of her wasn't surprised. "He's in there again?"

Todd nodded and stepped further into her room, partially closing the door.

"Music playin'?"

"Yep."

"Shit."

"You know he'll be out by the time *she* gets home." Her brother dropped his head for a minute, seeming in deep thought. When he lifted his head, he wore an inquiring smile. "Wanna watch *Medea's Family Reunion* wit' me? Or *Meet the Browns,* maybe?"

Todd did not want to watch a Tyler Perry play. Not really. He wanted to talk. Mallory knew that like she knew her name. It was an undercurrent of sibling understanding that only intensified after their mother died. "*Meet the Browns*—in *your* room this time." Mallory sent him an angled grin.

He smiled back. The tiny chip in his front tooth lent his smile a childlike appeal. He refused to get the thing fixed for some reason (some stupid "guy" reason, probably). He needed a haircut, though; Mallory thought his curls were getting unruly on the top. "I cleaned up the crumbs last time, girl."

"Yeah, but I had to remind you twice."

"Oh, but it's okay for you to keep wearing my Coppin State T-shirt, even though I've been asking for it for three weeks."

Mallory had to laugh; he had her on that one.

"Yeah, see? Uh-huh." With a smile, he left her room, closing the door behind him. She heard him laughing in the hallway.

Todd was gone and probably halfway down the stairs, but Mallory continued her guffaw. The joke had long ended, but she placed her hands over her aching belly (her stomach hurt, she laughed so hard) and howled even harder.

Hearing herself cackle, though, she paid closer attention to her laughter, wondering suddenly: what was so funny? She didn't have a concrete answer, but she had a general discussion point: something was wrong.

Wrong in an indefinable, scary way.

The joke had long ended, but the laughter coiled from the mild pain in her belly with a new purpose: she laughed to keep from crying. Not wanting to hear herself cackle again, Mallory forced her guffaws down.

When her laughter subsided, she sat back against her headboard and scanned her room again with a disapproving eye. The southwestern Aztec theme had to go. She thought about doing a more juvenile theme: maybe SpongeBob SquarePants or Black Barbie. Something like that.

Mallory tilted her head back with a sigh and watched the ceiling for several long minutes before closing her eyes. She laughed to keep from crying, but now, she wasn't laughing anymore; the urge to cry wanted its turn.

Something indefinable (and scary) was wrong, and Mallory worried. Worried for her father. Worried for her brother. Even for herself on some level.

But not for Ruth. Mallory wasn't worried for her.

If anything, she worried warily *about* her.

Todd used too much Dijon mustard, but not overly so; the sandwich tasted fine. He had the hang of their father's Dagwood recipe down pat. Mallory popped her last spicy-nacho Doritos chip into her mouth with her last bite of sandwich. The nacho spices provided an unusual yet tasty flavor combination. She savored that last bite before handing her plate full of crumbs to her brother.

She draped prone across the foot of her brother's bed while Todd sat on the floor beside his bed with his back resting against his nightstand. Taking the plate from her, he stacked their plates and placed them behind him on the nightstand.

Meet the Browns was on, but Mallory knew Todd wasn't watching it. Several of his favorite parts passed without him rolling on the floor in a giggling fit. She noticed he barely cracked a smile. When the part in the play came when Mr. Brown was "Slayin' in the Spirit," hitting folk in the head, and Todd didn't even grin, Mallory had had it. She knew he wanted to talk anyway, so enough with the preamble. She grabbed the remote and paused the video.

On the television, L.B.'s and Sarah's frozen video expressions were hilarious.

Mallory cracked up, surprising Todd. Her laughter must have gotten to him because he started laughing with her. She rolled onto her back, clutching her stomach, trying to catch her breath. This laughter was better than that episode alone in her room. That laughter battled some underlying fear and misery; this laughter was genuine and solely humor based. The two hooted for a good minute or two, with Todd's chortles dying out first.

Attempting to quell the giggles swirling in her throat, Mallory kept her eyes on her brother, using his serious expression to get the job done. Finally, her laughter diminished. She sensed maybe now he was ready to talk.

They were silent awhile.

Todd stared at her. "...Why does he go into the room like that, Mal?"

Mallory thought she might know but shrugged, thinking about Kelz's 'Generation Why?' comment. There were certainly many *whys* in their home that needed answers.

"He'd stopped for a while," he added. His perplexity knotted the furrows of his neat but thick brows. He shook his head. "It creeps me out." He turned his attention back to the television.

Mallory did, too: L.B. and Sarah remained frozen in mid-crazy expression. She turned back to her brother.

A hint of a smile creased his jaw, and she then noticed the amount of hair on his face. Her little brother needed to shave. Mallory's eyes widened. She couldn't believe she'd missed this before. "Todd!"

"What?!" He jerked his head her way, eyes wide with alarm. "What's the matter?"

"Your face."

"What about it?" His question was low, heavy, with more bass. The timbre of his voice dropped late last year.

Deeper voice, hair on his face, another two inches in height since June—her little brother was becoming a man at the speed of days (not years). Mallory wondered if any other aspects of manhood claimed him.

Todd stared at her with a look of part concentration, part apprehension, as if trying to read her thoughts, doing their sibling-communication thing. After a moment, he put on a shrewd grin before rising and sitting next to her on his bed. "And no, I'm not anymore."

She turned back to L.B. and Sarah. "Not what? And you'd better be." Mallory maintained her focus on the paused figures on Todd's television.

"Yeah, okay." He added a scoffing chuckle.

"...When?"

"This past summer: end of July."

She turned to him. "You don't have the date?"

He frowned. "Guys don't do that shit. Memorializin' dates is for girls."

"Whatever." Mallory sucked her teeth with a lip curl and looked away. Her little brother had one-upped her. She now doubted she could teach or tell him anything; her level of authority may have just dropped a notch in his eyes. She didn't want to be jealous, but... "Why didn't you say anything?" She was his sister, not his brother, but they were close: talking about sex wasn't new ground for them.

He bounced his shoulders, displaying uncertainty.

"So, you big man now, or what?"

"Am I acting the big man? You wouldn't have known if it wasn't for this conversation." He nudged her. "But I would've told you...eventually."

"So, who was it? Do I know her?" She wouldn't look him in the eye.

"...Divinia Watson."

"Oh, she's cute— Wait!" She whipped her attention to Todd and sat up more. "*Divinia Watson?* She's what, eighteen?"

"Not until November."

"Daaamn." Mallory gave her brother the once-over again, trying to step outside of being his sister to view him in a neutral light. She could only go so far with it. Todd was cute, becoming more handsome as he grew older (the facial hair helped), but he was still just 14. He could pass for 16, maybe 18, Mallory guessed, but Divinia *knew* Todd, so... *Ugh!* "So how did— I mean, has it been just the once? You wore a condom, right?"

"Nosy, ain't we? And, of course, I did."

"Oh, so now that you've popped your collar, we can't talk like before?"

He reached for his almost-empty glass of ginger ale. "I didn't say that."

"Okay then." Mallory waited.

Todd finished his soda and glanced at her sideways. He settled the glass back down with a sigh. "So,...you want the nitty-gritty or just the high-level?"

"Somewhere in between."

He sighed again and stuck his tongue in the space created by his chipped tooth; something he did when he wanted to concentrate or was lost in thought.

Curious as she was, Mallory changed her mind about wanting the details—at least for now. "You know what? That's okay. Save it for another time."

"Huh?"

"You heard me. Tell me about it some other time. I still wanna know your business; don't worry." She smiled teasingly at her brother.

Todd shook his head. "Women."

"Don't even try it."

He didn't seem to know how to respond to that, and Mallory took semi-selfish pride in shutting her brother up. Maybe she retained some level of authority after all. They sat silent until the pause button released and the cast whirled back into action.

This time, Todd grabbed the remote. He stopped the video, turned the television off, and then stared at the dark screen with pondering concentration.

"Done with the Browns?"

Todd didn't look at her. "You never answered my question."

"To reconnect with Mommy."

He nodded with deliberation and grew quiet again. When he spoke again, Mallory had to lean closer to hear him. "Daddy's got big money: from the inheritance, his art, his properties. He's got us. What'd he marry her for?"

They were talking about Ruth now. "I don't know, Todd."

"She doesn't even look like Mommy." He mumbled his words with frustrated anger. Todd finally turned to her. His eyes were wet, but he didn't cry. "And she's mean to me, Mal." He probably didn't want his voice to waver, but it did.

"She...did something? Is... Is that why you were on the roof the other night, in the rain like that?" Mallory stiffened with the memory, seeing her drenched dad inching toward her brother to avoid spooking him. Todd wasn't crying now, but he'd been crying then; the rain didn't camouflage it.

Her brother nodded, but his head barely moved.

That fear and misery knotted in her stomach again, and the air grew thick, making it harder to breathe. With no laughter to fight it off this time (nothing was even remotely funny at this moment), the fear and misery now coiled around the disgust, sympathy, and anger in her center, too. She wasn't cold, but she gripped her upper arms to pause her tremors of disquiet.

Ignoring the helplessness threatening to send her into a round of crying or laughing hysterics, Mallory stared at the dichotomy that was her brother.

Mr. Hairy Face (now two inches taller than she) had cashed in his V-Card.

But when it came to their stepmother, the unsettledness in Todd's eyes revealed how much of a little boy the almost-man really was.

Chapter 4

Signifying Nothing

T he Winthrops' first session progressed poorly on several levels for one main reason.

And, despite her love of the color and design of the oversized leather sofas and her linen-fabric tufted barrel chair, Dr. Naomi Alexander entertained the idea of changing her office décor and getting rid of the mustard-yellow seating group.

The Winthrops' first session.

Changing her office décor.

Those two notions were unrelated, but Naomi's attention to both was equal, and yet, (she knew) somehow tied to one another. A part of her couldn't wait for revelation of the connection.

Five people sat in varying postures on the yellow furniture, like poppy seeds on a lemon muffin. Five people sitting, one person talking. And talking. On and on for the last eleven minutes.

When Julia Winthrop died three years ago, Naomi knew then, after counseling Jeffrey, Mallory, and Todd, that her sessions with them accomplished little. She'd worked to get them through the initial shock of losing their wife and mother unexpectedly, but Jeffrey Winthrop stopped the sessions once Mallory and Todd started back to school. He stopped attending sessions when he began presenting symptoms of complicated grief.

Mr. Winthrop didn't mention any hallucinatory experiences back then, but his mourning for his wife persisted and intensified beyond simple depression. Her mysterious yet innate ability to see flickers of auric fields continuously informed her of Jeff's depression states. Those rare times his aura flickered for her back then: nothing but this dark, muddy, heavy blue, thick with woe. In those previous sessions, his yearning for Julia was poignantly lucid. He'd since remarried, but she expected more of the same with these sessions.

Her tolerance for her patients' varying afflictions waned as of late, but she did her job and did it well when treating people. Still, she reserved particular empathy and tolerance for patients struggling with losing a loved one. But, while Naomi very much wanted to redirect Mr. Winthrop away from his detour into a grief pathological three years ago, he'd ended the sessions, and thus her hands were tied. And now, a second chance presented itself.

Unbeknownst to anyone, along with auric sight, she also experienced what she'd termed *flashes of truth*: these acute hunches (at times with imagery) somehow, someway, grounded in truth. But she'd had no occurrence of a "flash" while counseling the Winthrops years back.

Naomi sat in her sizable mustard-yellow chair, facing her patients. She faced the leather sofa and loveseat, positioned in an inverted "L" across from her chair and in front of her office window. She entertained the idea of moving the sofa to the opposite side so that it faced away from the window but thought better of it. Often, that window served as an assistant of sorts, giving patients the distraction needed to gather their thoughts and open up when Naomi's professional approach reached a roadblock. So, she guessed, the office layout would stay the same, which left the décor—meaning the big-ass yellow furniture...

Jeff Winthrop sat on the sofa with his hands folded in his lap. He shifted attention between his children and the view outside, his baldpate gleaming in the late morning light. For a big guy with a tall, muscular stature, Mr. Winthrop's posture appeared prim. The folded hands indicated to Naomi: the man exercised control—doing what he could to keep it together.

Mrs. Winthrop (Naomi believed her name was "Ruth") continued talking.

Naomi shifted her attention from prim-looking Mr. Winthrop to his daughter, Mallory. Mallory sat beside her father in repose, looking very much like him, with copper-brown skin and deep-set eyes. She was a pretty girl, but her facial expression was not. Whereas her father did all he could to contain his emotion, Mallory sulked and did not disguise her displeasure. Whether that displeasure stemmed from being in therapy or from disdain for her stepmother, Naomi didn't know.

Mrs. Winthrop shifted in her seat, mentioning something about being on the deaconess board at her church.

Mallory rolled her eyes up in her head with what Naomi knew to be an internal sigh, thus solving the mystery.

Suppressing the urge to smile at her discovery, Naomi moved on to the youngest Winthrop. Mrs. Winthrop (*"Ruth," right?*) completed the trio on the sofa, sitting next to Mallory and rambling on about something or other, which left Todd with the loveseat all to himself.

Unlike his sister, Todd took cue from his father and appeared to be exercising restraint with a posture stiff but not prim. He sat across from Naomi, but his attention focused somewhere overhead and behind her. She looked over her shoulder to determine what held his attention. Her wall displayed framed prints of jazz artists and famous classical music composers, which occupied Todd's focus.

The wall once held her credentials, along with a plethora of awards and plaques of recognition. She'd since removed the filler and fluff and cut to the chase by taking down the awards and plaques and leaving only her credentials, which now adorned the wall behind the sofa opposite her office window. A proud alumnus, she took particular pleasure having her medical degree from Johns Hopkins University, centering her license and board certs.

That was all her patients needed to know anyway: that she was qualified, certified, and doctor-fied to treat them. If they needed proof of her success as a psychiatrist, evidence rested in the bottom left-hand drawer of her desk and on the bottom shelf of her corner bookcase.

Naomi turned back to Todd, who continued studying the pictures. Obvious tension stiffened the muscles along his jawline, and on further observation, his focus on the images wasn't as intense as Naomi first imagined. He didn't fidget or show outward signs of disinterest, so she wasn't sure if the boy exercised restraint or had mentally checked out of the session altogether.

Given his age, Naomi figured it to be the latter, but she had no way of knowing what was going on with any of them unless she got this session started officially. That meant *she* needed to be the one doing some talking—not Miss Talkity-Talk Winthrop (*"Ruth," right?*).

Naomi clapped once, creating a resounding pop. "All righty, then!"

All four Winthrops startled at the suddenness and volume of her interruption, but they each looked her way. Very good.

"Why are you here, Missus Winthrop?" Naomi asked.

"Call me 'Ruth,' please." Mrs. Winthrop offered a smile.

"Cool. 'Ruth,' then. Why are you here, Ruth?" Naomi didn't smile back.

It was instinctual and instantaneous: she didn't much care for this woman. Sometimes you *could* judge a book by its cover. There was something pretentious, underhanded, and unsympathetic about her, coming through something as ordinary as her smile and tone of voice. Liking Ruth, however, had nothing to do with treating this family, so Naomi would have to exercise some restraint herself (well, she'd manage an effort, anyway). At least she had the woman's name right.

With eyes holding a tentative expectancy, Ruth gazed at Naomi's unsmiling face. Yes, there was a touch of darkness about her.

After some reluctant milliseconds, Naomi offered a scant upward turn at the corners of her mouth.

Ruth seemed encouraged. "I'm here because several problems at home need to be worked out." She sat taller but didn't look at Jeff.

Mallory turned to Ruth with eyes narrowed.

With only a flit of eye movement in Mallory's direction, Ruth continued looking at Naomi.

Naomi dispersed her attention among the group.

During therapy with them three years ago, the Winthrop kids' auras didn't flicker for her, only Jeff's. And although they were young, the non-occurrence had little to do with their ages; she'd received aura-flickers from young children before and since. But it happened that way sometimes. Naomi didn't rely on her flashes of truth nor her aura-flickers—especially for treatment; it was a pointless pursuit at best.

The unpredictable nature of her flashes and the oft-changing nature of auras (and thus, her flickers) made the occurrences quite a loosey-goosey capricious experience. Her flashes were serious events (and not always dire), and her flickers were informative, but this was the thing: oftentimes, she experienced them when she didn't want to—and didn't experience them when she did want to.

She was a young college student when these talents awakened, and back then, she initially responded to the occurrences with the naiveté and awe her young age dictated. But youthful she was not anymore; she now responded to the events of her flashes or flickers with a casual indifference and acceptance as she would...walking, showering, or cooking.

But that was neither here nor there.

Discounting any supernatural or paranormal notions about her abilities (she didn't require use of a special camera to see auras), Naomi saw people as people, not their aura colors, so regardless of her flashes and flickers, what she relied on was her training and skill, her people-knowledge repository, her keen intuition. Today's session would be no different.

Todd watched his sister. Intense focus (absent earlier) seeped in.

Her eyes landed on Jeff Winthrop, and it surprised Naomi to find him looking back at her. His expression suggested he wanted her approval of Ruth's response.

The smile Naomi gave Jeff was genuine. Whether he surmised approval from her response was immaterial, but for the record, she sided neutral on the woman's response.

Naomi shifted her gaze back to Todd. "Why are you here, Todd?"

Todd's big, round eyes now focused on Naomi. She thought his soft curly hair, smooth pecan-colored skin, and big, caramel-brown eyes were enough to have plenty of 14- and 15-year-old girls blowing up the cellphone clipped to his hip. His facial hair likely drew the interest of a few older teenage girls as well, but rather than being cocky and full of adolescent hubris, the boy appeared reserved and vulnerable: traits more appealing than his aesthetic appearance. He shrugged and mumbled something suggesting the equivalent of "I don't know."

Completely satisfied with Todd's answer, Naomi turned to his sister. "And where are you with all of this? Why are you here, Mallory?"

Mallory kept her eyes on Ruth. "There are issues, yes, but I'm mainly concerned about my brother—and my dad." Mallory now turned toward her father, and 16 melted into nine.

Jeff Winthrop put a hand on his daughter's thigh and patted it with a light touch. He smiled at Mallory, but Naomi recognized authentic emotion bottled in the cords of his neck muscles. "Daddy's fine, baby." His voice offered feigned reassurance.

Mallory shook her head; she detected the pretense. "No, you're not, Daddy."

"Mister Winthrop, why are you here?"

"Call me 'Jeff,' Naomi; you know that."

"Okay, okay. But there have been some changes..." Naomi looked pointedly at Ruth, then back at Jeff, "...since you were here last, Mister Winthrop, so I wasn't sure."

"It's *Jeff*, Naomi." He smirked with kind eyes and a wan smile.

"Okay, well, *Jeff*, why're you here?"

Naomi's light sarcasm reached Jeff's funny bone. He chuckled briefly. However, the pain in those deep-set eyes revealed that maybe he'd rather be crying. Jeff put a knuckle up to one eye, and Naomi knew she wasn't too far off. "Yeah, there're some things needing attention, I guess. The incident with Todd tops the list..." Jeff nodded slowly as he studied the floor. He lifted his eyes to Naomi. "Yeah," he concluded, blowing a thin breath of resignation.

Naomi sat forward some. "We'll get into the roof incident in time. But okay. So: we have 'problems.' Right?" She ticked the index finger of her left hand and looked at Ruth.

Ruth nodded.

Naomi eyed Jeff and ticked her middle finger. "We have 'things,' no?"

Jeff nodded.

Naomi identified number three by ticking her ring finger. "There are 'issues' with concern. Yes?" Naomi focused on Mallory.

Mallory nodded.

Naomi turned to Todd. "And then there's simply 'I don't know.' Right?" Naomi ticked her pinkie finger to represent number four.

Todd nodded with a sarcastic smirk full of charm.

Naomi glanced at the clock. She'd allowed Ruth to go on too long. In any event, she needed to ask her customary question and keep things moving.

"Well, it seems Todd and Mallory are closer to their truths than their parents are. Now—"

"Parent," Mallory corrected. She didn't look Ruth's way, having made her point.

Naomi fully expected the correction—that it came from Mallory didn't surprise, either.

Ruth gave no facial clue Mallory's correction affected her, but her backboard posture lost some rigidness.

Todd gazed at his sister with pride—as if she'd voiced something he wanted to say. Naomi also picked up additional cues in his expression (something translating much less enthusiastic than unvoiced pride), and she felt sorry for him. Todd still grieved his mother's passing, but her sympathy sourced differently, beyond sadness for his loss.

She didn't bother checking for Jeff's reaction to Mallory's statement. "Well, before we explore the reason or reasons you all are here again, I'd like first to get a feel for everyone's—"

"Spiritual compass," Mallory finished.

Naomi grinned at her. "Remember from the previous sessions, huh?"

Mallory nodded, but Todd answered (with his own nod): "Yeah, I remember that, too."

Ruth shook her head. "I don't remember any religious questions on the questionnaire we filled out."

"Because there weren't any. I reserve those discussions for in-person sessions. It's a 'Doctor Alexander' thing. I can gain only so much from what's on those forms." Verily, she'd discerned quite a bit from her pre-therapy questionnaires, but no one need know that but her.

"I see," Ruth responded.

Naomi wondered if she did. "Okay. Well, who'd like to start?"

Ruth opened her mouth to speak, but Naomi had heard enough from her for the time being. She'd tuned out most of what the woman said, but she'd gotten the gist: God-fearing, church-going woman, realtor and property manager, deaconess board, etcetera, etcetera.

All of it, sound and fury...

Naomi wanted to hear from the others (those actually needing treatment), so she spoke before Ruth could get a word out. "Todd?"

If Todd's eyes could have widened any further, his eyeballs would have spilled from their sockets. "Me?"

Naomi plunged her chin in confirmation. Shades of gray and cranberry could work for her décor. She preferred the jolting brightness of her yellow, but the new colors offered a version of mood, too.

"Um, I believe in God, I guess."

"Your faith is your armor, Todd. You can't be guessing," Ruth stated.

Todd's posture sunk deeper into the back of the loveseat.

"If you're referring to Ephesians, chapter six, Todd's faith is his *shield*, which is only a part of God's armor. But thank you, Ruth. I got this."

There was nothing Christian about the scowl Ruth sent her at being corrected, but a wan smile immediately replaced it.

"Go ahead, Todd," Naomi prompted.

"I wasn't saying I guess there is a God. All I meant, was that if Doctor Alexander wanted to know how we felt about religious stuff and whatever, well, I believe in God. I said, 'I guess,' because I don't know how specific she wants me to be or whatever. I—"

"Todd," Naomi interrupted. "It's cool; your response was fine."

The gratitude in his eyes made Naomi that much more irritated with Ruth. Something needed to be explored between these two.

"You go to church, Todd?"

After a confirming glance toward Mallory, he nodded.

"Do you like church?"

"Sometimes."

"So, where you feel you are spiritually—is that working for you?"

He furrowed his brow with a hesitant smile. "Huh?"

"Never mind, sweetie. That's more of a question for your dad and Ruth...and maybe your sister." Naomi swiveled her eyes to Mallory.

"I'm non-denominational like my mother was. That's working for me just fine." She snapped, stopping short of sucking her teeth.

"Well, good for you. But have I done something to you? What's with all the attitude?"

"Sorry, Doctor Alexander," Mallory's voice rose and shook, "It's not you. I'm just—"

"Wait. Wait, Mallory. It's okay. It's my fault. Let me back up and initiate the session by letting Ruth know how things go. Okay?"

Mallory dipped her chin in hesitant concession.

Naomi turned to Ruth. "Ruth, as the rest of the family knows, with me, the conversation should flow. While I use my medical background in therapy, I don't use it to the exclusion of all else because I believe that regular, correlated time in the prudencesphere, using *common sense*, is invaluable in resolving some or even most basic forms of mental and emotional stress. To that end, conversation drives the sessions. Starting next week, I may take notes during the sessions or record portions of them. As you know, confidentiality rules the roost; my advice is to say what you want. Neither my approval nor opinion of what you say is of concern here. Okay?"

Still seeming bothered by their earlier exchange, Ruth nodded.

"Jeff? Mallory? Todd?" Naomi observed each of them in turn.

Each gestured their understanding and assent.

"Good. Now, let's get back to our spiritual compasses."

"Why do you ask about this, Doctor Alexander?" Ruth drew her burgundy Bottega Veneta hobo bag closer to her body.

Naomi refrained from giving her permission to call her by her first name. "Well, it will give me a better understanding of how each of you approaches death, grief, or mourning, as well as family conflict." She sensed family conflict at the heart of the *issues*, *problems*, and *things* referred to earlier.

"Oh, I see."

Naomi still didn't think she did. "Good. So now, how about you?"

"Well, as I said earlier, I'm a deaconess at my church, I'm on the youth ministry team, and I sing with the Praise and Glory Voices choir with my church on second Sundays."

"Okay, that's nice, but where are you spiritually?"

Ruth gawked as if to convey she'd already answered that. In other words, like Naomi was crazy. She frowned. "I just—"

"No, you recited a list of your church roles and activities."

"Oh." Ruth directed a scanning gaze at the other members of her family. "Well, my church is non-denominational with Baptist influence. I guess..." She tried not to look at Mallory but failed, sending a glance her stepdaughter's way. "I believe we are born with original sin and that the way to the Lord and Salvation is through Jesus Christ."

"Mmm..." Naomi nodded noncommittally.

Mallory sucked her teeth.

"Is that working for you, Ruth?" Jeff asked.

Ruth's lips parted with a slight startle, as if surprised Jeff spoke.

Naomi wasn't shocked at all.

Ruth fixed her eyes on her husband. "Yes, Jeffy, it is."

Now Jeff sucked his teeth, his brow bent with annoyance.

"What, Jeff?" Ruth appeared hurt, but a tad annoyed herself.

Naomi didn't want to hear Jeff's answer to Ruth—not yet, anyway. And she didn't know about Jeff, but Naomi thought that nickname, "Jeffy," blew chunks. Blew huge, saccharine, trying-too-hard chunks. The moniker sounded forced, sappy, unfitting, and false. But maybe he liked it. "So, Jeff: your turn. Let's hear from you and round this thing out in a tidy knot."

Jeff offered a small smile. "You're something else, Doctor Alexander."

"So I keep hearing. And stick with 'Naomi,' Jeff. Okay?"

"Okay. Yeah, um..." He sat taller and cleared his throat. "I, uh, I don't know, Naomi. Like my son, I believe in God, but here lately..." He paused, shaking his head, and then let out a sigh. "I don't know where I am on a spiritual level. Believin's all I got for you right now. And to be honest, no, it's not working for me, before you even ask." A knuckle came up to that eye again.

"I hear you, Daddy," Mallory uttered.

"Yeah," Todd added in a volume equating a whisper.

Ruth looked as if wanting to add her own supportive comment; her lips worked, but no words came out. An initial expression of sympathy on her face transformed into irritation again. Naomi then noticed Ruth's green eyes: a shade the color of Cerignola olives. How that physical feature escaped her notice before, Naomi didn't know. Maybe it was distraction derived from all Ruth's other sound and fury...

"Do you believe in an afterlife, Jeff?" Naomi asked quietly.

"No," he responded just as quietly.

"So, you don't believe in spirits and such?"

"My wife is dead, Naomi." His tone was stiff, final. But his eyes held what Naomi best guessed to be hope—that just maybe he was wrong.

"No, your *wife* is right here, Jeff." Ruth's expression was almost stern. The woman could have offered her statement more gently, but clear defiance came across instead.

Mallory sucked her teeth. "Oh, whatever!"

It was all Naomi could do not to laugh. Sometimes professionalism proved a pain in the ass. Jeff's response, though, killed the giggle rising in Naomi's throat.

"And *why* are you my wife, Ruth?" Jeff's voice cracked, but his eyes burned with an anger overtaking the torment in them seconds before.

Naomi's desire to laugh shifted into intense curiosity. *What did that question mean?* She held her tongue and tensed, waiting for Ruth's response. In the edges of her vision, Naomi noticed Mallory and Todd waited likewise; their father's question surely stirred a level of apprehension.

Ruth glanced at the others in the room before fixing a glare on Jeff. "No, you didn't." She didn't do a neck-roll or a finger-wave, but the inflection in her tone exposed her urban upbringing. Bible quotes would not fit in at this particular juncture.

Jeff held her gaze, unmoved by her change in tone and disposition. "Why are we married, Ruth?"

"Because we love each other," Ruth answered. Again, the gentleness of the words did not match her tone.

"Bullshit," Mallory muttered.

Jeff snapped his focus to Mallory. "Unh-uh, M-Sweet."

"But, Daddy—"

"No."

Mallory checked the resoluteness in her father's posture; his demeanor ended further debate. She mouthed, "Sorry," and sat back.

Jeff turned back to Ruth. "There is love, yes."

He means there is love now, but that doesn't mean there was love in the beginning, Naomi determined. And whatever love there was now, she doubted it was the good, Black love he shared with Julia. She saw nothing between Jeff and Ruth even approaching it. "Okay, beautiful people, this is obviously a topic for a later session. I'd like to get everyone back on track with the focus of today's session: spiritual compasses." Listening to herself, Naomi almost wanted to howl again. *Spiritual compasses? What the hell?*

Jeff sat up, sniffed, and drew a hand down and over his face, stretching his jaw muscles. "You're right, Naomi." He stared out the window. He was clean-shaven now. Jeff was handsome, but it was an odd look for him. Three years ago, he sported a mustache and beard stubble.

Todd lifted his posture, too, as did Ruth. Mallory seemed to slink deeper into the cushions; sitting between her dad and stepmother was not the best choice.

"Good. Now,..." Naomi watched Jeff, seeing the pain creep back into his eyes, witnessing the grief settling over him once again.

Except for the faint ticking of the wall clock, the room hushed. Periods of silence were normal and frequent, even beyond the first session.

"I miss my— Julia, Doctor Alexander." Jeff's furtive glance at Ruth appeared to suggest apology for his admission, but Naomi believed he started to say *my wife* again (instead of *Julia*). Jeff cleared his throat.

"And believing in God or an afterlife is not helping me deal with what's here, what's *now*. I—" He let out a heavy sigh and tilted his head back, watching the ceiling for several seconds before closing his eyes and letting out another sigh. He shook his head against the sofa cushions. His movements sounded a wispy crunch against the sofa's leather upholstery. "I... I— I can't," Jeff started, "I— I can't..." No longer shaking his head, he stared at the ceiling. A tear trailed into his right ear.

"Then don't," Naomi replied. Professionalism aside, she wanted to hug the poor man. "Then don't," she repeated. "At least not today." It would come soon enough.

"'The grass withereth, the flower fadeth: but the Word of our God shall stand forever,'" Ruth recited softly.

For Naomi, the tone was right this time, but the words sounded out of place. Isaiah, chapter forty, was ideal biblical reference for the discouraged, but Naomi thought the first verse, '*Comfort ye, comfort ye...* ' may have been better to recite. "Thanks, Ruth."

Ruth nodded, eyes somber and mouth glum.

Naomi thought the gesture a bit too theatrical. *Maybe I'll use grays and blues for the wall and linear black furniture—something sleek and contemporary.*

"Doctor Alexander?"

"Yes, Todd?" Naomi didn't forget the boy was in the room. She paid close attention to his reactions to the discussion. She'd expected, however, for him to remain silent for the remainder of the session.

"Do you pray?"

"Yes, I do."

Todd nodded—it was answer enough for him.

Naomi didn't pursue it further; it was answer enough for her, too.

"See, Todd: even Doctor Alexander lives by the Scripture. She's a God-fearing woman. See?" Ruth regarded her stepson with a direct, pertinacious gaze.

Naomi watched Ruth nod her approval but resisted clarifying anything for the woman, at most glad Ruth didn't use her first name. "In light of what your stepmother said, I want to say this to you, Todd: when people determine they're going to follow scripture or live the life they preach or teach about, it should be a happy decision, and they should be happy doing it. We refer to biblical scripture as 'the food of life,' right?

But when it's done with angst or regret, or done halfheartedly, or for sake of appearance, what's the point? Get what I'm saying?"

"I think so," Mallory replied.

Todd nodded his understanding as well.

Naomi hoped Ruth wouldn't come back with anything. She returned her attention to Jeff. "You okay, Jeff?"

"Yeah, I'm good." Jeff lifted his head, looking around at the others. "Sorry about that."

"It's cool, Dad."

"Yeah, Daddy. We understand." Mallory patted her father's thigh. "We miss her, too."

Ruth leaned forward, reaching across Mallory for Jeff's hand.

Jeff waved her off. "I'm good, Ruth. Seriously."

The glower Mallory shot Ruth should have vaporized her.

Jeff's semi-rejection appeared to bother Ruth, but she recovered with a not-quite-there smile as she turned to Naomi. "So, you have a problem with people trying to live spiritual lives, Doctor Alexander?" Her tone was neither defensive nor challenging.

There were times, though, when Naomi thought she engaged in dialogue with her patients a tad too much. "Well, these days, being 'spiritual' is more like a trend or club thing, with people using the term with more rigid connotations. And it's more alienating than welcoming. It's not everyone, mind you, but lately, with those I've run into, that's been my experience." Naomi paused. "But to answer your question, I have no problem with people trying to live spiritual lives. We should all do that—to the best of our ability."

Not that Naomi cared, but Ruth seemed satisfied. Her olive-green eyes scanned over Naomi before taking in her office, pausing now and again on the furniture. She returned her attention to Naomi: "You know, Naomi, for a therapist, you seem to have chosen the wrong colors for your office, don't you think?"

"Meaning?" Naomi wished Ruth had stuck with addressing her as "Doctor Alexander." She could tell Ruth she preferred she didn't use her first name, but it could cause problems that might hinder helping the other (younger) Winthrops.

Mallory swept her gaze around the office while Jeff ran a hand over his head, trying not to look embarrassed.

Todd glanced at Mallory and shrugged. He then took interest in the loveseat, giving it a level of observation it didn't deserve.

"Well," Ruth continued, "I've had basic psychology, so I know enough to know that yellow represents cowardice."

"Yeah, and...?" Naomi had suspicions about Ruth's inquiry, but she wanted her to say it. That semester or two of introductory psychology apparently ranked high for opinion-giving and psychological analysis and interpretation. Naomi wondered what she suffered through ten-plus years of medical training for then, when a semester or two of Psychology 101 would have sufficed.

Mallory dropped her head with a snicker.

Jeff and Todd channeled their concentration out the window, Todd chewing his bottom lip.

"Yellow also represents happiness, positivity, energy, optimism, enlightenment, remembrance, honor, and joy, Ruth. So, what's up? What's this got to do with anything?" Jeff kept his attention on the view outside.

She wants to get a dig in, Jeff, that's all. Maybe bring me down a peg or two, too.

"Nothing, Jeffy. Just saying. As a realtor, I see many model ho—"

Mallory blew a breath with her eyeroll. "And *nothing* is yellow?"

Ruth cut her eyes at her stepdaughter. "Don't be smart, Mallory."

Todd's attention zipped to his sister, checking warily for her response.

Mallory postured as if she wanted to come back with something, but after a glimpse toward her brother, she altered course with a suck of her teeth and shake of her head.

"Let it go, Ruth," Jeff advised with succinct weariness.

Naomi watched and listened to this exchange with mild indifference. The exchange helped some, however. How interesting that Ruth would comment on her office décor when Naomi was thinking about changing it. "Well, beautiful people, we need to wrap this up. This was par for the course for a first session. Aside from the grief and mourning needing to be worked through, other dynamics at play here also require exploration." Naomi eyed everyone but Ruth as she spoke.

Indeed, not very professional. She'll try to do better.

Ruth and Mallory stood, ready to leave. This dull but deep magenta shading emanated around Mallory for quick seconds before disappearing. It suggested Mallory experienced the negative vibes of red or blue energies. Perhaps the anger or impatience of red, but Naomi believed Mallory harnessed more of the burdens and depressive thoughts tied to bluer hues. Understandable.

Naomi stood as well.

The menfolk appeared hesitant to leave, as both remained seated a few seconds longer. Jeff chuffed a light chuckle as he looked over at his son. "Well, man, I guess we'd best prepare for departure, too. The ladies seem eager to call it a day."

Todd smiled at his father. "Yeah, I guess we'd better."

Father and son shared another look before rising from their seats.

Naomi wished she knew what that look meant.

"Okay then." Naomi looked up at Jeff, extending a hand to him. "Same time next week?"

His curt shake possessed a solid grip. "Next week."

Naomi turned to Ruth. With her eyes, Naomi invited confirmation for the next session.

Ruth nodded with an I-guess-so shrug.

"Next week, Doctor Alexander." Mallory's smile spread too wide.

"Todd?" Naomi asked.

Todd gestured toward the others. "Well, I'll be in the car with them..."

Varying degrees of titters followed (Todd included).

Naomi preferred ending her sessions on a positive note, but somehow this rendered a hollow victory. She let it pass. "That'll work." She headed back to her desk. "You all take care. Be safe."

The Winthrops echoed assorted goodbyes and were gone.

Naomi sat at her desk in her still-considered-strange ergonomic chair (the thing *was* ugly, but it helped with her posture). She wanted to reach for the flask in the back of her desk drawer, but dismissed the thought. Although the session with the Winthrops (well, *one* Winthrop in particular) gave her enough cause, she was on a new tip nowadays.

Or trying to be, anyway.

In response to a comment by former patient Rick Phillips, Naomi was doing her best to limit how often and how much she drank. So instead of going for her flask, she opened a cabinet door of the credenza behind her and retrieved a bottle of raspberry-flavored tea. She was a regular hot tea drinker (varied herbals a delight), either during session or while reviewing a case, so this tea indulgence was simply a new take. Naomi guzzled thirstily, wondering how Rick was doing. She kept regular contact with him, and since she planned to visit him in the coming weeks, she guessed she'd find out then. Her visits with him, although still exploratory, were also becoming these relaxed exchanges, more caring and friendship based.

The raspberry and tea flavors mingled and danced in her mouth with a refreshing jolt. It wasn't necessary beverages be cold; Naomi preferred bottled waters and juices at room temperature. Her thirst slated, Naomi focused on summarizing the Winthrops' session for their file.

Someone knocked on the door.

"Yes?"

The door opened. Dr. Imani Greene, Naomi's resident physician in training, poked her head in. She smiled as she held her spring twists back from her face with one hand. "Willette Hargrove's file is ready, Doctor Alexander. And Vivian Phillips left a message for you to call."

Speaking of Rick... "Thanks, Imani. I know you'll be glad when you can email me or leave a voicemail, huh?"

Imani stepped into the office further. "No. I like that you require us to interact with you. Digital communication has its place, but for our line of work, interpersonal skills need to be worked on at every opportunity."

Imani reminded Naomi of her daughter, Leslie. "I at times think so."

"I'm on the Masterson case study, but if there's something else..."

Naomi imparted a full smile. "Are you campaigning for the Best Resident Assistant of the Year award, Doctor Greene?"

Imani smiled back. "Nah, Doctor Alexander. I just—" She shrugged.

Naomi snickered in fun. "I may have another task or three for you, but I have another resident to help share the load, so I can't ignore him, now can I?" She patted a folder on her desk. "But I'll tell you what. Let me wrap up the session summary for the Winthrops, and you can draft a preliminary profile for me to review. How's that?"

Imani shook her head at a considering pace. "Doctor Alexander, we're not supposed to..." she trailed off, eyes on Naomi with eager anticipation despite the cautionary reminder.

Naomi gazed back, her expression calm.

Imani returned a big smile. "Thanks, Doctor Alexander!"

"Not a problem." She wished Imani could address her by her first name, but protocol dictated otherwise (for now, anyway). "Now, go. Masterson awaits." Naomi shooed her out of her office.

She returned to the Winthrop file before the door closed.

Naomi relied on her medical training for therapeutic approaches, but psychiatrists also utilized select manuals to support or guide their process. Three sources were always in her reference rotation: the *Diagnostic & Statistical Manual of Mental Disorders* (DSM); the *Applied Behavior Analysis Advanced Guidebook: A Manual for Professional Practice* (ABA); and handbooks or volumes published by the American Psychological Association (APA). She kept copies in both offices. Naomi considered some of that reference reading now.

Grief. An emotion with such elusive properties, the boundaries defining its manifestation were so obscure as to be nonexistent. Unlike depression or post-traumatic stress disorder (PTSD), the clinical arena for grief had its starting point and then just kind of...dissolved. Grief, however, was a valid emotion, and Naomi used her firsthand knowledge of it when trying to help patients. Not that she no longer grieved herself, but she'd come a ways—it depended on the day. Some days she'd come further than others, but there were still days grief held her in its crippling grip as much as it did moments after those policemen arrived at her house five years ago. As it did bedside in a little boy's nautical-themed bedroom eight years before that.

Naomi stared at the Winthrop file data for some seconds, lost in thought, before straightening her shoulders and allowing the words on the page to make sense again.

Contained grief reflected aspects of depression and PTSD in that the symptoms lingered. The symptoms, if left unresolved, could become protracted then traumatic, leading to complicated grief. Complicated grief could result from normal bereavement, in which case the sufferer needed more than the usual comfort and support.

Naomi was reasonably sure Jeff Winthrop was experiencing some form of complicated grief, but only more sessions would bring this to light. If indeed complicated grief was the case for Jeff, it would be atypical. Jeff's records didn't indicate any history of depression or anxiety disorders.

Unlike the APA and the recent-edition DSM, the ABA manual didn't officially establish a standard diagnosis of complicated grief. Still, Naomi entertained the idea of utilizing traumatic grief therapy for the Winthrops, using cognitive-behavioral and interpersonal techniques. This approach should mitigate Jeff's (and thus the family's) trauma and relieve stress, but Naomi remained somewhat iffy on the whole imaginal exposure part of the therapy with this case.

If Jeff was having hallucinatory experiences, Naomi needed to find out. This particular PTSD symptom would most likely stem from Julia's death being premature.

Naomi continued writing notes on her legal pad for another twenty minutes. She rarely used her digital recorder (go figure). When she finished, she reviewed what she'd written and shook her head.

It all sounded good on paper. And maybe she'd rely primarily on her interpersonal techniques. Because when all was said and done, Naomi still had her common-sense diagnosis: Jeff had some issues, yes, but basically, Ruth had to go. No in-depth analysis needed. Naomi, however, needed to treat this family for their grief as well as move them along to that realization.

"...And why are you my wife, Ruth?"

Naomi finished the file prep work; she could give it to doctor's-pet Imani. She stood and surveyed her office, taking in the décor.

Cranberry? Grays and blues? Something old-fashioned? Something sleeker and more contemporary?

She put her hands on her hips, trying to decide. She'd conducted her session with the Winthrops while considering a change to her décor, suspecting the two were related.

"I've had basic psychology... yellow represents cowardice."

Naomi scoffed and took her hands off her hips. She picked up the Winthrop file and headed out the door.

The yellow furniture and everything else stays.

Fuck her.

OB: Pause Button

- What's the real story behind Jeff and Ruth getting together?

- With all the tension between them, does Jeff ever discover how Ruth treats Todd?

- How does Mallory navigate the tense situation?

- What will Naomi's approach be (since she clearly has a problem with Ruth)? And what's the deal with that odd dream involving Leslie?

So glad you want to know more!

Answers to these questions (as well as other interesting events occurring as the story takes place) await you inside the tale, in digital and bound formats at book retailers online!

Get *Obscure Boundaries*:

I'll see you after "The End."
Up next: a preview of book 3, *Broken Benevolence*...

Broken Benevolence

Book 3

Prologue: "A White Christmas"

(Two Years Ago)

G ingerbread.

That's what this smells like.

And pine. And burned bacon. Blood. Urine. Holly.

But oddly, mainly, this horror smells like...gingerbread.

Everything happened so fast. And now, time moved at a glacial pace.

Why... Why does blood smell metallic? Like...licking a rusty nail?

"Ma?!" That was followed by a heavy moan: Chelsea.

Marcus made no sound, but she could help no one.

Metal. And gingerbread. And pine, and urine, and...

Pain was everywhere and nowhere. She couldn't isolate where she hurt worst or even hurt exactly—uncertain if that was good or bad.

Does it smell and taste so metallic because of the iron in it? The copper, maybe? And did someone turn the air conditioner on?

The thirty degrees outside slinked inside. Growing colder by the second, she wondered why she'd be pondering such unimportant things when the pain in her ribs and the subtle but continuous feeling of draining away throughout her everything else told her not to mind such trivialities: she'd be dead soon.

"Ma?! Please! Someb—!" Chelsea again; her moan an almost rallying cry of painful hopelessness.

Rustling movement and footsteps overhead.

Someone dropped their keys; they landed next to a crushed gingerbread square. In the glow of the twinkling Christmas tree lights, she saw letters on a maroon crescent-moon keychain before a glove-holding brown hand (a Masonic ring askew on the pinky) picked them up. The ring had tape for a better fit. The carpet, soggy now with bodily fluids from her and others, squelched as Carhartt work boots passed her. Mesmerizing hues of red, yellow, and green bounced off the odd-shaped scuff on the left boot before it disappeared from view.

The devil's in the details.

She wanted to laugh at that. And why was Marcus so quiet? She stared at the Christmas tree (the twinkling colors offering their support) and tried to remember if they fried more bacon after burning the first round. She tried to rise, but pain (crisp, sharp, and unforgiving) halted everything.

Staring at the Christmas tree lights was better.

Repeated clicking and beams preceded distinct buzz-whir sounds. Distinct...but she couldn't place it.

Larimore popped into her mind and was gone just as quickly.

"Is the bitch dead?" A sadly familiar voice asked this question with such hopeful anticipation; she experienced pain having nothing to do with her plethora of physical injuries. Familiar, too, was the staid cologne scent now mingling with the blood and urine and pine and gingerbread.

"Lickety-split," came the answer in a voice that might have been familiar (the phrasing peculiar) if the gingerbread and blood and pine and urine smells (and the fading-away sensation) didn't keep interfering.

No response to Mr. Lickety-Split.

A trained swimmer back in the day, she still had skill with holding her breath and used it now. She stared straight, moved no muscle, and made no sound for fear of having the question answered with force in the absolute affirmative.

She thought she heard Chelsea moan again, but pain throughout her own body was in furious debate with the fading-away sensation, the winner yet to be determined.

No fading, Cecily. Focus on the lights...and pray.

Red (closer to a pinkish) and blue and white and green and yellow... Much better.

Someone cleared away the condoms.

Another of them then cleared the duct tape from over her mouth, snatching it off with unfounded, unnecessary, and confounding malice, creating a new source of pain spanning the front of her face—but she could breathe so much better now, breathe over and around the blood in her nasal passages (suffocation probability: reduced).

"White Christmas" by the Drifters played on and on from the CD player in the kitchen, adding a note of seasonal cheer. Thinking she heard sirens, she prayed within as she focused on the lights, thanking God for her many blessings, praying for the well-being of her children, and—

Is... Is that blood dripping from the bulbs? From the tree? My blood?!

She laughed then. Laughed through the pain, not caring if she was heard, and helped along to her doom (a much better relief compared to this).

She laughed and worried for her children as the pain began losing the debate with her consciousness.

Cecily laughed as she faded, thoughts of the Gingerbread Man dancing in her pained head...

He didn't know what the fuck was so funny.

How could she be...*laughing?*

Her laughter died as emergency responders arrived, sirens blaring.

Dammit. Who called the—?

Chest burning and stinging inside and out, he reclined, resuming the position, and waited.

He fumed over the turn of events but began planning anew.

Chapter 1

Southern Belle in the North

S he liked the cold. And the quiet. And right now, each endeavored to make her feel welcomed. The cold made you go inside yourself for warmth. The quiet? Well, nothing to do in the quiet but think.

Cecily slowed her already slow walking pace.

No hurry to get home. Not today. Not on the anniversary of—

There were anniversaries of births and marriages and career service achievements. And anniversaries...of other things.

"It doesn't feel like two years." She startled at the sound of her voice breaking through and against the thirty-nine-degree day. The temperature was above-freezing but didn't feel like it. MIA for two days now, the sun allowed an uncharitable pall to cast upon the withering lawns and chilly sidewalks. The air itself was...gray.

She was a Southern belle in the north: Cleveland didn't get cold like this. Cecily pulled her handkerchief from her coat pocket and dabbed her tearing-from-the-cold eyes.

Two *years*? The question (both asked and answered) sat in her throat, threatening to choke her with the realization that, yes, although it didn't feel like it, it had been two years since the home invasion.

And yet, another winter of discontent.

Cecily sent her gaze forward: about a mile before reaching home.

Oscar called her a nut for getting off the bus so far from home. Said she was a nut for taking the bus back and forth to work—especially with an Infinity Q70, a Nissan Maxima, and a newly restored 1967 Cadillac Deville convertible parked at home. Oscar called her a nut (and other names, too) for a lot of things.

The Deville was hers, however. To do (or not do) with as she pleased. Even Oscar didn't have the keys—and that felt good. It was her piece of happiness.

"Larimore's gonna love it." She whispered the words as if she weren't alone on the street, and gumminess formed behind her eyelids as her heart sank. She was far from home (and not the home waiting at the end of her walk). Cleveland, Mississippi: *that* was home.

Or it used to be.

As small as it was, she missed her family. She needed to call Kyle, too. Only older by two years, he sometimes acted like he was her father. And although Daddy died when she was 18, Kyle was 20, and Larimore was 16, their father (and Mama, too) did a fine job raising them to that point. At 44, she didn't need Kyle's guidance. Cecily grinned against the cold; maybe it was time to visit him.

Kyle wasn't visiting her. Not while she was married to Oscar. Kyle loved Roland. But Roland...was gone.

Fighting tears (it was just too cold to cry), Cecily wished for a hat (although she wouldn't wear it for fear of messing up her hair and pissing Oscar off), and her stupid contact lenses irritated (although she could see fine without them).

Besides, tears would not bring her dead husband back.

She shifted thoughts to her Deville and her younger brother's utter joy once he laid eyes on it (*if* he ever laid eyes on it). Larimore was up for parole soon; there was hope.

She sat on the bench in the mini park, taking her usual time to prepare for going home. She did her best to forget what day it was, but she wasn't one of the lucky ones—and an elephant never forgets.

Two years. Or was it just yesterday?

Refusing to allow tears to freeze on her cheeks, Cecily wanted her parents in a way she hadn't wanted (or needed) them since she was a child. But a train wreck left that option defunct.

Why are you harping on all this stuff? Because it's the anniversary?

She focused on a sparrow, pondering the answer.

His eye is on the sparrow...

Cecily startled as the bird took flight. She needed to get home.

Wonder what's happening at the Ellis? The Arts and Jazz Festival's coming this spring...

Her mind here, there, and everywhere, she didn't feel good; feeling much like one of her "episodes" (as Oscar called them) coming on. She dreaded them but couldn't help them, either. The episodes left her drained and confused, and so...*angry*.

Not this time. I don't care what day it is; I won't this time.

Her grandson's tiny, innocent giggle filled her head, and Cecily smiled despite the cold. Maybe she could get away for a little while, visit Marcus and her grandson (named Roland after his grandfather). She missed her son, but like her brother, Marcus wanted no part of her marriage to Oscar. And after being beaten and shot when those men invaded their home two years ago (today), he also imposed and expressed his protest by moving away and staying away. Oscar wasn't his father, and he didn't like him, her son often told her, so there was no need in faking the funk. And, embracing his adulthood at 22, Marcus faked no funks. He and his Uncle Kyle got along splendidly. Marcus's dislike of Oscar aside, Cecily missed her son.

Chelsea (now 20) left the house after her rape and assault two years ago and never looked back. And although she sided with her brother on many of his views about Oscar, Chelsea was less expressive with her protest, displayed more tolerance and understanding. Still, she stayed away—and Cecily missed her daughter, too.

She once worried Oscar had somehow abused them, but Marcus and Chelsea were adamant he hadn't. She reassured them their inheritance was safe, couldn't be touched by anyone but them. Marcus and Chelsea weren't concerned about the money, either; they had complete faith in her and the handling of their financial affairs. They simply didn't like Oscar, didn't like her with him.

Her children were adults, couldn't be convinced of Oscar's merits, so discussions about him didn't happen. Oscar had good qualities. He did. Although her children disagreed, marrying Oscar benefited her. In the end, Oscar had her best interests at heart.

No one else would want her, anyway.

Oscar had his fair share of trials, of failures and successes. He tried hard, too. You didn't just walk away from that. Oscar wasn't always the nicest person and could be downright mean sometimes, but she wasn't perfect, either. You take the good and bad in marriage. After six years of marriage, taking more of the bad was presumable.

You didn't have it bad with Roland.

She didn't have it bad now, either (did she?). Cecily sighed. She didn't feel good: anxious and headachy.

Two years.

The case had grown cold. Although they had DNA samples, nothing more had come of it. It surprised and saddened her: despite advances in forensic and crime-solving technology, cases still went unsolved.

Despair threatened to surface, and Cecily almost went with it. It was a daily struggle *not* to give in. Not to just run into the waiting arms of Miss Madness and find a bizarre peace and solace only she could give. But there were her children to consider, and her grandson, and Oscar.

Go home, Cecily. Just go home.

She should, and she would.

Your flowers can't be out here like this, Cecily. Take them inside.

Cecily glanced down at her fingers curled around the green foil paper enclosing fresh flowers. She'd forgotten she had them. They could be fickle with her (sometimes lasting weeks, other times, just days), but she liked fresh flowers, no matter the season.

Flowers are perfect for acknowledging anniversaries.

Cecily shut her eyes. When she opened them again, she watched a squirrel scurry across the street, another following, right on its tail. Perhaps they were hurrying to get out of the cold.

She'd given the police what she remembered: the keychain, the scuff on the boot, the missing brooch (a high school graduation gift from her mother; it was the only thing they took, but one of the many things that hurt). But it wasn't much, so they couldn't do much with it. Oscar even reported a name he thought he heard them call out as they moved about the house that night, but again: nothing.

And she was left with nothing, too: nothing but the pain of what happened to her family, nothing but...episodes.

Cecily sat, missing her home in Cleveland, missing Marcus and Chelsea, missing Roland.

Sadness, intense and full, stabbed her middle with thoughts of her dead husband. She'd spent sixteen loving years with Roland "RC" Cooper, bore him two children, and then...brain cancer gave them *in sickness and in health* before finally opting for *till death do us part*. He'd been gone almost ten years now, and while her memories of him softened with time, her love for Roland and the sadness over losing him didn't.

"Oh, Roland..." Cecily watched the condensation of her breath in the cold air disappear—much like Roland did from her life.

It was cold. Just downright, no-wind-chill cold, *stiff* cold (unusual for early December). Sitting still on a park bench made it even colder.

Cecily didn't move. She breathed in the frosty gray air, gazed into the gray day, and didn't move. This wasn't her usual quiet moment of respite taken before doing something. Today, this anniversary day, sitting on the bench was different. She so didn't feel good.

Maybe I'll stop in to see Janyce first.

Janyce (with a "Y," not an "I") was the closest thing she had to a friend up here, so Cecily guessed Janyce was her best friend (although, at 44, do you have "best" friends anymore?). She met Janyce Mabry soon after she and Oscar and the kids moved into the neighborhood (and befriended her soon after that).

Cecily liked Janyce because she was loud and materialistic. Janyce wasn't a good listener, but she was an excellent distraction, so the tradeoff was fair enough. Janyce's husband, "Hank" (his real name was Carson, and although curious, Cecily never asked why he had such an odd nickname), was a quiet soul much like herself, with this bass of a voice making people take pause sometimes when he spoke. He was such a sweet guy, and Cecily, for the life of her, couldn't figure out why he ended up (or even stayed) with Janyce. But she said nothing: to each his own and all that.

The Mabrys were childless, and Cecily sensed that while Hank would've welcomed a son or daughter (or both), Janyce wasn't interested—because she didn't want to share. Being a parent meant sharing your blessings with them such that, if you could, you one day afforded them a life better than your own. But Janyce liked her things and her Hank: sharing either would be problematic for her.

Oscar wasn't interested in having children, either, having abandoned his parental rights to his daughter, Keisha. Keisha was grown, living in Germany, but Cecily ensured the lines of communication remained open. Oscar couldn't have cared less. He said he was too old to have children, but in the deepest parts of herself, Cecily believed he didn't want to share, either.

Advances in medicine made it possible for women, even in their 50s, to have healthy babies, but Cecily was far past the baby-having stage of her life. With Oscar six years her senior, given his view of age and having children, he was way past. It mattered not. And when she interacted with that deepest part of herself? It was all for the best.

If Janyce's silver Mercedes sat in the driveway, she would visit and extend her respite. She could sit with Janyce and listen to her tales of shopping adventures and merchandise returns, of upcoming travel plans and holiday party plans...and lose herself long enough to forget (if only temporarily) what today was.

Cecily doubted Janyce remembered what this day was; she too often suggested Cecily forget what happened, leave all that in the past.

Headachy sensation frolicked at her temples, and nausea wanted to play, too, flitting around to tease her stomach. The gray cold introduced itself to her bones as she sat on the park bench, but Cecily stayed put. Even the promise of warmth inside the Mabry home couldn't get her moving.

Not yet. She liked the cold.

All this mind-wandering interfered with a memory trying to surface. A memory the police could do something with. A memory to free her...

Cecily focused, trying to obliterate thoughts of Cleveland and Kyle and Larimore and train wrecks and Roland and Chelsea and Marcus and little Roland and Oscar and Janyce (and even "Hank"), to allow the memory to burst through.

It wouldn't.

It was there; Cecily sensed it circulating her subconscious. But it was cold, and she didn't feel good. Frustrated and fed up with her unsuccessful attempts to release it, the memory turned tail on her, moving in the opposite direction, burrowing deeper in her mind.

Desperate, Cecily willed the memory forward, wanting it to stop messing with her already and illuminate the darkness, *her* darkness. "Please...?"

A tiny puff of condensation winked at her before vanishing into the gray cold.

Not to be cajoled, the memory stayed put in the recesses of her mind.

Cecily stayed put, too, thinking of nothing and no one in particular, just wanting to feel better. The no-wind-chill cold added a mild breeze to its fun, sending wafts of pine to her nostrils. Sometimes the whiff of pine gave her the creeps, made her afraid and weary.

Times like now.

Janyce's house.

"Yes!" Cecily got moving.

Alas, the temporary asylum of the Mabrys' family room (or kitchen) wasn't available: although her car was in her driveway, Janyce wasn't home. Cecily's disappointment numbed her; she couldn't move at first. Her legs stubborn and uncooperative, she stood on the Mabry porch.

Today just wasn't her day.

Or maybe it was precisely her day.

Legs finally working, Cecily made her way the few houses down to her own home. She gripped the wrapped stems of her flowers tighter, thinking of playing a little Nina Simone to quell her nerves, maybe listen to "Mississippi Goddam" on repeat—it was a violent protest song, sometimes soothing her when it didn't...ignite her.

She paused in her driveway, feeling better as she ran a hand over her "Devin," once more hopeful her younger brother would get to see it soon.

The 1967 Cadillac Deville convertible pushed its interesting blue against the hateful grayness of the day (its paint wasn't royal-blue or cyan or a sky-blue, but a combination such that only "interesting blue" sufficed). Cecily took her keys out of her bag (Marcus had the other set) and got inside, relishing the new-leather smell. She worked hard to restore the car and had a ball doing it. "Devin" (her improvised derivative of Deville) was auto-show ready, but having the car finished also meant the distraction was over.

Take it for a spin. Don't go in there yet.

"Saturday," Cecily promised herself (and the steering wheel). Now having something to look forward to, she nodded with excitement and confirmation, thinking of riding with the top down in the bitter cold. "I need to get you in the garage, though, boy; this isn't cutting it." She got out, leaving Devin to sit and chill (literally) in the driveway. No, her car wasn't a "girl," and Cecily liked it that way.

Why doesn't Oscar have a set of keys?

"You know why." Cecily headed for her front door, entertaining it no further.

She entered the house, the alarm beeping to announce her presence—and then everything went wrong.

The music: wrong. And the smells: all very, very bad and wrong. Oscar smiled at her as he approached from their kitchen, a plate of gingerbread squares in his hand.

And then everything (the whole awful lot of it) was happening again.

Cecily didn't remember going into the closet, but there she was (the coattails brushing against her said so), and she wasn't leaving. She didn't bother to turn on the light, preferring the dark. She wasn't going out there. Out there with the wrong music and the wrong...*smells.* "White Christmas" by the Drifters insisted on traveling through her covered ears. She thought she screamed for the music to stop, but wasn't sure. Oscar talked to her through the door, asking what was wrong, asking if she was okay. She screamed for him not to open the door, not to let those things (the music and smells) in with her.

Pine and holly and burned bacon and urine and gingerbread and...blood.

... She'd just finished putting the leftovers away, trying to figure out the best way to get the odor of burned bacon out of her home, when a loud bang from the front of the house sent her that way, fear knotting her insides. She had time to see her front door hanging open, to wonder why the alarm didn't sound, to see someone in a ski mask and wearing dark-blue heading through their living room, when white pain crashed through the back of her head.

...Screams. Chelsea. Those screams cut short. Cecily's eyes fluttered open. Her head felt the size of a pumpkin and had the pain to go with it. Someone was on top of her, grunting and breathing gingerbread breath on her; an erection hurried in and out of her passage. Her screams bounced against the duct tape covering her mouth and ricocheted into her throat; the binding plastic ties dug into her wrists. More men took turns with her in the rape-train, saying such vulgar, unnecessary things. She checked out, sending her mind somewhere, *anywhere* else...

...Rustling from somewhere upstairs, a gunshot, and then another. Chelsea?! Marcus?! Oscar? The last man finished his business, pulled away, and then a boot (black and just big) rammed *into her torso from her left. Another slammed into her head from the right. And then...nothing.*

"Please..." Cecily pleaded into the dark closet, wanting everything to stop. The headache teasing her temples as she sat on the bench earlier now exploded in her head, threatening to take up permanent residence. The tang of bile surrounded her, but the putrid stink didn't add to her distress. It wasn't a bad smell. Not like those others. "Please..." On her knees, Cecily rocked in place.

...Sharp, vicious, critical pain seared her abdomen, bringing her around in time to see the blade leaving her body. Her face throbbed in atrocious magnitude. She'd also voided her bladder at some point. In a haze of pain-filled vision, she observed several soiled condoms around her. *Several!?* The cold from outdoors flooded in from the busted front door, but it was warm compared to the iciness filling her body. Nothing from Marcus. Faint moans from Chelsea.

Staring at the Christmas tree, *Cecily faded again;...the darkness much better than this.*

The closet door opened despite her protests, and although the music stopped, Cecily could still hear it, still smell, not just the gingerbread Oscar made, but the pine, and holly, and—

"Ma'am?"

Curled into a ball on the floor, Cecily didn't move or speak.

"Just help her, man!" Oscar liked to bark orders when he was impatient (or bored).

"Sir, if you'd step back."

Oscar scoffed, but Cecily sensed him stepping back.

A hand touched her shoulder. It was a kind hand, but she cringed away from it still.

The hand left her.

Images from that night wouldn't let her go, but she couldn't keep company with the wrong music, bad smells, and depraved people. Help was here, just like it was back then.

Wasn't it?

"Ma'am? ...Cecily?"

"...Yes."

"Cecily,...can I help you up?" This voice was soft and caring but distinctly male.

Cecily felt herself nodding.

"I'm going to touch your arm now. Is that all right?"

Cecily allowed the gentleman to help her stand, but she wouldn't open her eyes.

"Ma'am, are you ill?" A woman's voice: caring but also annoyed.

"What th—? She's got vomit all down her clothes and on the floor. Of course, she's ill."

"Sir..." The tone (from the man) implored Oscar to shut up.

Cecily opened her eyes, wavering some with the light hitting them, but Mr. EMT held her steady at the elbow.

"Take it easy, ma'am," Miss EMT cautioned. She was tall and slender, her hair in a tight bun at the top which arched her eyebrows.

Cecily shifted her gaze to Oscar.

He had that look: the one appearing concerned and nervous, but with eyes reading the opposite. His mustache twitched with disapproval.

She may pay for this later. This was her third episode in as many weeks. They came more frequently since Thanksgiving, but Cecily didn't know how to help that.

Her flowers lay on the floor, delicate petals scattered, some crushed. Where was her bag?

Cecily looked at Mr. EMT (cute, late 20s, mediocre nose). "I'm okay now. Just need some water..." But she trembled still, and something in her eyes must have told Mr. EMT she wasn't okay at all.

He shook his head. "Ma'am— Cecily, I'd like to check your vitals."

"Len...?"

"Len" eyed Miss EMT (her badge read: "Donella") and nodded.

Hours later, Cecily lay in a hospital bed, trying to follow the documentary on television (a fascinating exposition on the Hershey company), doing her best to fight the effects of whatever sedative they administered. She failed miserably (and didn't dream at all).

She awoke, surprised to find it was the next day. The day *after*. The anniversary was gone.

She should've felt better.

Cecily signaled for her nurse.

It was mid-afternoon by the time she could freshen, eat (not much), and have her consult with Dr. Englewood.

Possessing a suitable bedside manner, he was a tall beanpole of a man with a slender, pinched, weak nose. He reminded her of Ichabod Crane. She and Oscar listened as Englewood recapped her medical condition (physically healthy but underweight) and prescribed alternatives to help her mental state.

Oscar went on his rant about her having seen a psychiatrist before, how nothing helped, how doctors get paid much money for a bunch of *I-don't-knows* as diagnoses and not helping people.

Cecily said nothing, in part agreeing with her husband. She'd spent months under the psychiatric care of Dr. Lewis, resulting in little more than a few venting exercises and several prescriptions for drugs with names most couldn't pronounce, and she had never filled. She was none the worse for it, but none the better, either: the "episodes" continued.

Dr. Englewood listened to Oscar's doctors-are-quacks tirade with only the tiniest hint of annoyance in his brown eyes before he nodded acceptance of Oscar's right to have an opinion. Englewood continued his task, asking her questions before entering something in her chart. He understood when she couldn't remember much of what happened while in that closet yesterday, let alone what happened two years ago.

She kept the things she did remember to herself: it was all too muddled to make sense—and she had enough people thinking she was crazy. In the end, Dr. Englewood couldn't force her to do anything. She was of sound mind (essentially) and not a threat to anyone (thus far).

When Oscar left the room to take a call, Dr. Englewood placed a brochure on her side table and a business card in her hand. "Sometimes, the *second* time's the charm," he'd said, his eyes imploring her to take his medical advice.

Cecily nodded, unsure what she was going to do (if anything).

Dr. Englewood and Oscar passed each other in the doorway, the doctor offering Oscar a customary parting shake of his hand.

Oscar didn't stay long (or *couldn't stay*), but Cecily chilled, allowing her mind the rest it needed. She called the office and informed Josh she'd be out a few days. She talked with Chelsea and Marcus and updated them (only half-listening to Marcus's leave-Oscar speech) before enjoying the delightful babble of her toddler grandson on the phone.

It was quiet, and she wasn't doing anything other than completing another page of the Jumbo Word-Find book a nurse kindly offered, when Cecily put her pencil down and reached for the brochure and card she'd placed on the side table without giving much additional thought. Joshua's "Get Well Soon" balloon and his flowers rested on the table, too, and a wisp of breath bottled inside her chest with her upturned lips at them.

Setting the card aside, Cecily reviewed the brochure first.

The brochure was for a psychiatric facility in Virginia, with pages of copy full of soothing words and marketing jargon to get you to sign right up. Cecily put it down, uninterested. She picked up the business card.

She expected more information than that provided.

Dr. Lewis's card was Crayola-blue with white lettering (tiny swirls and curly-cues in each corner)—and a neat little three-line tag about his services on the back. Cecily remembered his card being rather busy, so she expected more of the same from the card in her hand.

But looking at it, Cecily guessed the essentials were all that mattered. Cream-colored with black sans-serif lettering, the card provided rank and file: name, occupation, office address, phone number. No sales copy on the back to convince you to call, no tagline with calming, cajoling words to persuade you. The only flourish (if you could call it that) was the psychiatry symbol in the upper-left corner. Not with the Greek symbol for Psi and the infamous caduceus down the middle, but with Psi and the Rod of Asclepius down the center instead.

People commonly recognized the caduceus (with its two snakes and wings) as the symbol for medicine, but the Rod was the correct symbol. She didn't know why she kept track of such trivia in her head, but it was sometimes useful—like now.

Cecily stared alternately at the name on the card and the Rod of Asclepius (with its single snake winding a staff—no wings). This card was for another psychiatrist: this one female.

The name?

Dr. Naomi E.M. Alexander.

Chapter 2

The Best-Laid Plans

H e called her "Cicely" instead of "Cecily" by honest mistake. But she corrected him (who cares if rightfully so?), and he was determined to break her. Determined to break her little uppity, Southern-hick ass and leave no doubt. He grew to love her, too, but the breaking,...*that* had to come first.

She was from Cleveland, Mississippi. Who the fuck knew? The only Cleveland he knew belonged to Ohio. Average height, slender, nice butt, small but shapely tits, hair she forever wore in a ponytail—until he broke her of that, too. She was one of those bright, intelligent, speak-soft-ly-and-carry-a-big-stick types of women—until he put a dent in that line of thinking, reminding her: the only "big stick" she needed be concerned about was his. Her first husband ("Roland": such a sissy name) was a punk for letting her get away with such nonsense.

Didn't matter he was dead: a punk's a punk, dead or alive.

She brought some of that Mississippi up to the DMV with her.

That accent still fluttered through her speech (when untouched by an occasional stutter), driving him crazy. He couldn't stand it but tolerated it because Cecily was a catch. Her pretty face and nice bod made her a hot catch. Degrees in two majors from Delta State University made her an intelligent catch (he planned to finish and get his associate degree soon).

But the kicker? The bomb-ass motherfucking kicker? Her financial bottom line: $17.2 million and growing. He didn't know that soft-spoken, bright, funny, pretty, Southern hick carried the motherlode—until he snooped and peeped her financial statements while she went to the store. They weren't three months into the relationship when he discovered that delicious tidbit. Smart girls sometimes did stupid things: like leaving their information readily available. Well, it wasn't all that readily available, but one should take extra precautions: you never know whom you're dealing with.

Oscar slunk further into the cushions of his recliner.

A rerun of one of his favorite shows, *Housewives of Atlanta*, was on, and he was missing all the cleavage and trash-talk. That's the only reason he watched: the cleavage, booties, and the trash-talking—but foremost, the abundance of cleavage. Women being women.

But he was missing it on account of being annoyed—because something went wrong two years ago. Science and luck joined forces against him. The angle of the knife penetrated deep, yet missed every major artery and only nicked some organs. Cecily was a slender woman: there couldn't have been much room to miss anything. She'd even had bleeding on the brain from Carl's and Brickey's kicks to her head, but she pulled through it all—just fine. Chelsea and Marcus, too. What the hell? He didn't understand it; the plan was perfect. Home invasions were up in their neighborhood then; it should've been a lock.

Not getting his usual thrill watching Atlanta tits-and-ass, he switched to the Game Show Network (GSN); he liked a good game show. Except for *Jeopardy!* That show was for pompous assholes with nothing else to do but know trivia about shit like seventeenth-century dynasties and European geography. He rarely got an answer (Oh, excuse me, *question*) right on that lame-ass show (had to be rigged); no point watching it.

Oscar shifted in his seat.

He should be at work (Cecily returned to work days ago). But he used the excuse of his wife being in the hospital for all it was worth. It was only seasonal work, and he didn't have paid time off, so his check would be lighter come payday. That was okay: they didn't need the money—Cecily had plenty. His wife was a nut for working when she didn't have to, but the more she earned, the more there was in the kitty.

She said working was fulfilling or some other women's lib bullshit, but he didn't ride her about it. Let her work, shit; it also kept her out of his hair. He only worked the little he did to keep up appearances.

That's all women needed: appearances. Times they gave you the finger-wave-and-neck-roll full of attitude (something Cecily never did;

it wasn't her style): you beefed up said appearances to make it seem like their views mattered, to appease them. Simple.

All that mattered was keeping them quiet and the pussy coming.

Oscar wasn't a fan of *Deal of the Century*, but it was on, so he watched it. The show schedule during this part of the day was whack; the good stuff came on later. He had his lineup for programs of interest: cop shows, game shows, reality TV (the Black ones because they always gave up the T&A), and shows with judges named Judy. He got a kick out of that one, especially. Got a kick out of seeing how the woman believed her views of life (accented with a Yiddish expression or two) were universal, almost biblical. She was a joke—and the joke was on her; she had to use toilet paper like anybody else. He couldn't imagine her playing hide-the-sausage; it just didn't compute. She made bank, though; he'd give her that. Yeah, he saved time to watch the shows with judges named Judy.

He had other interests besides television, had some things going on. He had a few network marketing opportunities in operation. Those were lucrative if you worked them right; he hadn't found the formula to make it work for him. It was only a matter of time. People enrolled in his downline—he just didn't know what it took to get them to make him money. He sent them to the local meetings for that motivation jazz but still had little to show for it: a couple hundred dollars here and there. It had been five years; another three to five should have him set.

He also planned to get those last few courses behind him for his associate degree. He could knock them out, but hadn't been in the scholarly frame of mind.

Anyway, he had some things cooking; he was moving and shaking. Everything just needed to gel.

Thirsty, Oscar went to his fridge, grabbed a Corona, and drained it, standing before the cool air of the opened fridge cooling the basement's sixty-seven-degree warmth. He used the empty bottle to close the refrigerator door and tossed the bottle into Cecily's stupid recycle-bin (getting full). He'll take the container upstairs later. Oscar spat a loogie into his spittoon (which Cecily hated, and he enjoyed because she hated it so much) and went to his desk.

He kept his desk neat because order and organization were important. Even if those two things failed him two years ago, Oscar believed nothing good came from disorganization and chaos. His desk stayed neat to detect anything out of place. He wasn't worried about Cecily (she knew better), but that son of hers...

He didn't keep the good stuff near his desk (that would be stupid), but in the utility room: in a cashbox in the hole of their sump pump where he'd affixed a tiny shelf in there special. It was perfect; no one was sticking their hands down there. Floorboards and air vents and ceiling tiles, sure, but not sump pump holes.

Oscar retrieved the cashbox. At his desk, he examined the contents as *Deal of the Century* ended and an episode from the original *Family Feud* aired: time for a block of that Hatfields-McCoys game show with the hillbilly theme song. That Richard Dawson was a trip: getting his jollies kissing every female contestant. That irritated him sometimes, but he held no grudge; *Family Feud* ranked suitable entertainment: he always came up with the top five survey answers.

Oscar stared at the contents of his box: wads of cash, the To-Do list, Polaroid shots from the event (he still jerked-off to them sometimes), and samples of Cecily's handwriting. He stared at the To-Do list: a folded sheet of yellow legal pad paper, portions of the edges frayed and discolored with blood (*red and yellow make orange!*). He unfolded it, giving a cursory review and rundown, trying to see if he missed something. Nothing. Nothing missed. Except for the part where somebody called 9-1-1. *That* he hadn't counted on.

Annoyed, he refolded the list and returned it to its spot. Holding on to this stuff was stupid, but he couldn't let it go. Not yet. Otherwise, he'd been careful not to slip up. It was why the case went unsolved to this day. They had some DNA, but matches weren't in their databases—and wouldn't be. His men walked the straight-and-narrow, not so much as a parking ticket. They were smart men, patient. They knew what was at stake; Oscar didn't have to worry about any weak link.

Yeah, it was the best-laid plan, almost perfect, but *almost* didn't cut it, didn't give him what he needed. The perfect plan would've ended differently. They did a good job, though. Almost too good. He still had the scar from the bullet wound; they just missed his carrot artery. So, not a complete job, but a good one, and all would get paid well for it.

Oscar watched a commercial for a holiday auto show, images of classic cars whizzing by. He scoffed, thinking of Cecily's car. It was show-ready, but *he* couldn't show it. Cecily could, Marcus could, but he couldn't. That was one area he had yet to break her, but he'd let her have that little piece. She cared for that car better than she did him most times, but what the fuck: you had to give them something to make them think they had everything under control. He had his year-old Nissan Maxima, access to the Q70. He didn't press the issue over the Deville because it would *all* be his one day.

Well, not everything. Cecily's jerk of a son had a baby now (a son named after his punk granddaddy), so Marcus's money would go to him. Nothing to be done about that. It irritated him to no end, but whatever. Cecily's children didn't have access to their money until age 25; there was still time, motive, and opportunity (he watched a bunch of crime shows, too) to accomplish his goals.

He'd already convinced Cecily to have the papers drawn up, naming him powerful attorney in case of her death or mental incapacitation. He likely already had that right as her husband, but he didn't want to leave anything to chance. Cecily's asshole brother, Kyle, was always in her ear, trying to foil his plans, but ultimately the papers were drawn, signed, and delivered (Cecily took care of it herself). *So, fuck you, Kyle.* He had Cecily good and primed, so he wasn't worried; he didn't even bother reading all that mess.

There was also a special little something called life insurance; in effect since close to the day of their marriage and thus vested some years ago, the date of incontestability long passed. All that was needed was working the new plan carefully.

None of this is love, man.

Oscar sent that nattering little whiny bitch voice away with a scoff. He loved Cecily, but he needed to move on (he wasn't the family man he made himself out to be), and he wasn't leaving all that money behind. Bitching-up now only made matters worse, leaving room for mistakes. He did love her. But things were different now.

Besides, Cecily knew none of this. He kept Cecily under control, but he was good to her. Good to her, for appearance's sake (although he meant a good deal of it). It was too complicated to think about too much. Bottom line: his dear wife had to go.

Physically or mentally: made him no difference.

A picture of Cecily rested on his desk, and Oscar flipped it over, rubbing his chest to soothe the uncomfortable full feeling there.

He'd spotted Cecily at different times over several weeks before meeting her face-to-face in the laundry-item aisle of Walmart. He liked her looks from jump, but she always had her teenagers with her. They belonged to her; he knew that. The boy (a handsome young man) looked like her, and the girl (a hottie already) favored her mother, too. Since single women loved Walmart, he made Walmart his "shopping" grounds as well. Delia had just kicked his ass out and to the curb (there was no breaking that one, after all), and he'd suddenly found himself on the desperate side (something he loathed). He had an apartment again (month-to-month) using some of the money he filched from Delia and the bit of savings he accumulated working seasonal gigs, but that money wouldn't last forever. He could've stayed with some buddies, but to catch another female, he needed to have his own place—at least starting off.

Appearances were everything.

Prettier than Delia, the woman also seemed to have a desperation about her as she shopped, but he couldn't be sure. He couldn't have been sure about anything unless he talked to her. The teenagers left their mother to shop elsewhere, so Oscar took his chance. He usually shopped for *single* without the *mother*, but they were teenagers and almost grown, so practically the same thing. He didn't do toddlers and preteens: they needed too much of your time, needed too much...of *you*. It was why he made no slip-ups in *that* department. Well, there was the *one* slip-up: a daughter, Keisha. But she was grown now and living in Germany, last he heard. The baby mama knew better than to expect child support from him, and so handled all that on her own. He was okay with it. Kids weren't for everyone. And, at his age, kids surely weren't for him.

He wasn't one of the tall ones, but for all intense purposes, he wasn't bad looking (enough women confirmed that much for him). He could stand to lose a few pounds (he had a Corona-belly forming but not yet full-grown), but he wasn't fat. Delia always said he had a "talk to me" face (whatever that meant), so once he saw the teenagers leave the lady by her lonesome, he approached, watching her browsing the fabric softeners. He'd nodded his hello, she smiled back, and he saw that maybe *desperation* wasn't right, but *vulnerable* came close.

One month later, he moved into her townhouse. It was only a matter of weeks before he had her thinking she was madly in love.

Another month and he discovered the motherlode.

They were married five, six months after that. He'd changed his life (for the much better) in as little as seven months.

A few months into the marriage, she corrected his accidental mispronunciation of her name.

Breaking her didn't require violence (not intense violence), but a perfectly timed expression of something unexpected, unusual, and okay, with a dash of violence thrown in, did the damage necessary. He'd already drawn her in by then, worked on many of her vulnerabilities, so when his words rolled off his tongue with slithery precision to bring her uppity, hick-ass down, words emphasized with a severe, prolonged pinch to her side, the shift in their relationship solidified (point: Oscar).

When he hit her, he used punches sparingly—and never to her face.

"I think that's when that sometimes-stutter started." Oscar nodded. Yeah, he was pretty sure that's when it began. Or soon after another good pinching bruise or two.

She wasn't in love with him. He knew that. Cecily probably didn't know or realize it, but he did. But breaking her and owning her didn't require that. It only required having enough love to nurture the appearance of being in love. Cecily loved him. He loved her. That was all you needed right there. Just enough.

Her love for her children, that maternal crap to protect them, kept her from revealing the real to them. Cecily took part in keeping up a few appearances herself. They never liked him; he knew that, too. Chelsea liked him maybe a little (and he found he wanted her approval on some level), but the son: no happenings. But Marcus and Chelsea were teenagers then, involved in many teenaged activities, preoccupations, and distractions, so Oscar managed the situation well.

"She actually called out that punk's name." Cashbox in hand, he reclaimed his seat, remembering how Cecily called for Roland while she was in that closet, going through whatever the fuck crazy shit she was going through in there. Oscar seethed with the memory, but just as quickly, he grinned. He didn't expect the gingerbread to send her over like that. He expected something, hoped for something (she'd been showing signs), but not to *that extent*. Oscar chuckled as Richard Dawson explained the dollar values were doubled.

He planned to continue messing with her now-fragile mind, keep her unsure, unfocused, and...unhinged. Marcus and Chelsea stayed in her ear, but since they pretty much abandoned their mother after the invasion, Oscar could work his magic to his benefit. He didn't drive her over the edge hard and fast; these things had to be done delicately. Cecily going over the deep end full throttle didn't have the right look; it didn't show well. Appearances were everything.

Movement from upstairs: Cecily.

"Os-Oscar?"

He muted the sound on the television. "Yeah. What's up?"

"Nothing. J-Just wanted to remind y-you to call Odessa b-back. I'm headed out, r-run a f-few errands. G-Get some flowers."

Her and those damned fresh flowers she insisted on setting in a vase on the kitchen table. He wondered if he should "water" these, then decided not. He'll get the next bunch.

"N-Need anything?"

He sometimes made her specify where she was going, but not this time. The trick to it all was keeping her unsure of when they had to play that *other* game. "Nah. But...feel like making Crepe Suzette?"

Oscar grinned with the ensuing pause; no, she didn't feel like it.

"That's fine, sure."

"A'ight. Then I'm good."

"Oscar, d-don't forget your appointment w-with Doctor Halim's c-coming up."

He didn't forget, and he dreaded it: bad news sometimes came in ones. "Yeah, I remembered. Be careful."

"O-Okay. Shouldn't be m-more than a few hours: b-back by five-thirty at the l-latest."

Oscar grinned again. He didn't ask for a time frame this time, either, but her cooperation was appreciated—and expected.

"Cigarettes?" she asked as if hoping the answer was no; she'd been trying to get him to quit for years.

He had quit for this last week—because he had that appointment with Halim. "Nah, I'm good."

"All right." She closed the basement door.

He turned the volume back on just as Dickey Dawson asked them to "put another twenty seconds on the clock, please."

A few minutes later, he heard the alarm setting and then the Deville starting up; she was gone.

"I should've gotten 'going out' approval, though." He sometimes made her get prior hair-and-clothing approval before she went out alone; a show of control he exercised more in the early part of their relationship but still did from time to time. He made it appear rooted in love for her and making sure she looked good (which made him look good).

She mentioned calling Odessa back.

He'd rather not call his sister back. They were just going to argue-without-arguing again. It was the core of their relationship, and he wasn't in the mood. Let her do that mess with their baby brother.

Odessa didn't like him, anyway; he was hard-pressed to believe she loved him. The only emotion he sensed from his sister was disappointment. But even that was better than what his little brother broadcast toward him: contained distaste. Otis went so far as telling him that, as an older brother, he was nothing to look up to.

Instead of using his family nickname, "OJ" (for Oscar Jerome), Otis changed the meaning to "Old Joke," having good laughs at Oscar's expense. Since the OJ trials of 1995, Oscar dispensed with the nickname altogether, preferring people stick with "Oscar." Otis, however, still called him "OJ" sometimes when he was in one of his moods.

His siblings didn't respect him in the least. These days, he barely talked to them, let alone saw them. And maybe all that hurt somewhere inside, but Oscar didn't dwell.

Odessa and Otis thought they were better because they had college degrees, some status in their communities, and always got their snide digs in to remind him of his lesser status. He was the oldest, yet he carried no weight with his siblings (Otis even made it a point to ensure visits to their parents down in Florida didn't overlap by more than a day). It got to the point he and Cecily stopped going to family get-togethers because he couldn't afford the damage to the finely tuned appearance of a different persona he'd refined to land Cecily (and all the others). And besides, Odessa liked to correct him too much: correct his grammar, his word usage. He didn't have a bachelor's degree, but he had gone to college (he planned to get that associate degree next semester, maybe); she didn't have to show him up so much.

No, he wasn't calling Odie back anytime soon.

What about you stealing from them? Totaling Otis's car? And that four-thousand dollar "investment" Odessa and your parents couldn't afford but afforded you? How about—?

"Shut up. Whatever, man. Okay!?" He hated thinking about his family. A lot of that wasn't his fault. Oscar rubbed his chest, grumbling, "Shoulda been a policeman," to the dark basement (smelling faintly of the fading ocean-breeze air freshener Cecily plugged in last month). Policeman, detective; *that* would've had some miles on it: the uniform, becoming detective, knowing about cases and shit on local crimes, the life-risk factor. He'd been a security guard for some years; he would've been a cinch to make officer.

Being the black sheep of the family, he didn't have his family's love and support (they didn't even care about his recent heart problems), but once he had Cecily's money, Oscar knew all that would change. Blood was thicker than water, and money couldn't buy love, but what money could buy (and influence) was sometimes just as good—even if only the appearance of it. All he had to do was stick with the plan.

Plan A didn't pan out, so he was on Plan B. And if Plan B didn't work out... Well, there were twenty-six letters in the alphabet.

Plan A morphed into Plan B; the mental-incapacity angle was less messy. Dr. Lewis's sessions, because they didn't help, only gave Cecily a deeper sense of despair, which worked in Oscar's favor. The notion she was incurable reinforced the idea something was seriously wrong with her. When she stopped going to Dr. Lewis, Oscar stepped in to help. The little things were enough: like a plateful of innocently baked gingerbread squares.

So now, here they were, getting ready to do the whole psychiatrist-bit again. It fell in line with his alternate, less-violent plan, so he would go through with it—for appearance's sake. However, he didn't have the most comfortable feeling in his gut for this go-round. He couldn't put his finger on it, but something about this next go-round made his insides all watery and jittery.

It wasn't because this Dr. Alexander was female; that mattered least to him. Women were women. She had the same weak spots as all the other split-tails, and he'd exploit those weak points. She could be broken (most could). But (and he didn't know why exactly) he didn't feel good about going to her. They could always change doctors.

You should leave this all alone, man. Think of your health.

Oscar shook his head in answer to himself; he was too far in it now. And although he didn't take those pills Halim put him on (like he was supposed to), he was fine, felt good (today, anyway). And well, aspects of these plans for Cecily amused him. Aspects...aroused him.

For the tiniest moments, Oscar wondered if he was okay, if he was sane. But before any deeper consideration, his attention shifted to give the fifth most popular survey answer, his anxiety over meeting Dr. Alexander all but forgotten.

Chapter 3

Christmas Presents

R elying on the use of her right hand put her in a weird mood, but given the pain in her left wrist (even with the brace on), Dr. Naomi Alexander realized she'd have to manage.

She'd manage because part of her was also excited. There were big plans for this afternoon. She also had to read up on a new patient scheduled for next week, but that was later.

Adjusting to the awkwardness of using her right hand as she held James Baldwin's *Go Tell It on the Mountain*, she read a few passages to a group of elderly residents at Garden Meadows, a senior-citizen facility in Laurel, Maryland. She usually volunteered her services here every other Tuesday, but today was Friday.

Naomi read to her audience, scanning them as the words flowed and wondering if any instances of her auric sight or visionary abilities would ignite. She'd termed these talents *aura-flickers* and *flashes of truth*, respectively. Her flashes of truth manifested as acute hunches (sometimes with imagery) somehow, someway, grounded in truth.

As she read, she saw traces of reflection in the men's eyes, as if relating to the tale of John Grimes in Baldwin's semi-autobiographical novel. The women, too, wore soft, thoughtful smiles as she read, nodding at certain parts. So much history in the room. So much wisdom and experience (albeit touched by the effects of age and illness). Filled with pride over her audience, Naomi sat straighter, read with more conviction.

Still and attentive, a few of their auras soon flickered for her at random, some in tandem. Most of those few flickered in solid shades of teal, fuchsia, or pumpkin-orange (Christmas season be damned), and some... Well, some of those auras were quite faded. Fading auras were a sad occurrence, but Naomi didn't tarry.

Garden Meadows was an older, more rundown facility, but the staff kept the place clean and airy and, as the Christmas holiday approached, quite festive. Mistletoe, garland, and twinkling lights hung throughout the rooms reserved for social activities; the aromas of pine and cookie dough commingled in the early morning holiday atmosphere. In the kitchen: homemade cookies baked in preparation for the upcoming Christmas party.

Along with the aura-flickers, Naomi experienced a flash of truth about one of the staff. In it, she saw staff aide, "Jontavious" (oh, these names), wearing a lab coat and performing lab duties. She didn't know Jontavious well, but in her flash, he chuckled while working in earnest with a coworker, and Naomi was pleased for him. Jontavious wouldn't be working for Garden Meadows much longer.

The thirty-degree range chill in the air last week had warmed to a comfortable fifty-nine degrees, but that didn't detract from the cozy holiday feeling of the room. Naomi sat in front of the most enormous Christmas tree she'd ever had the pleasure of sitting in front of. The tree was massive: just big and green and colorful.

She exercised caution using the fingers of her left hand to push her glasses up the bridge of her nose and read more of Baldwin's prose. She finished the selection for today's reading, to the soft claps and words of praise for her reading style and appreciation for taking the time to read to them. They looked forward to her visits—as much as Naomi looked forward to visiting.

The alternate Tuesdays she worked with the crew at Hardluck Rebound, feeding the homeless. Years ago, she left Hardluck Rebound and switched to Abiding Ways for her charitable efforts. But she didn't like the vibe at Abiding Ways and much liked the people volunteering with Hardluck Rebound, so she returned to them and never looked back. Reading to the elderly at Garden Meadows was her solo charitable gig. Money was fine to give, but people didn't realize their time was just as valuable (if not more).

Naomi exchanged hugs with some of her reading group members (holding in a grimace of pain every time someone bumped against her brace). She said her goodbyes, breathing in the varying and sometimes competing redolences of perfumes, colognes, soiled incontinence pads, and analgesic creams. She'd next see them the Tuesday after New Year's when she resumed reading *Go Tell It on the Mountain*.

Before she left, they presented her with a gift-tin of York Peppermint Patties, along with two woolen hats (likely inspired to keep her head warm in the winter months). During her visits, many of the senior ladies commented on her short hair, fretting she'd catch her death of cold. Common colds came from viruses, not cold weather per se, but you didn't debate with history, wisdom, and experience. Little did they know, her hair was longer than it had been in years.

While heading to her car, the excitement returned, making her stomach fluttery with anticipation. She had a few errands to run to keep her mind occupied, including calling Mark to confirm execution of the plan.

She had four hours to fill.

The wait was going to be torturous.

Naomi drove with composure despite her desire to test the limits of her new BMW 540i and speed to her destination. Reluctant to let go of her beloved X5, she traded it for a new silver X5 and bought a metallic-blue 540i sedan to meet her other driving needs. She sometimes missed her first X5, but the new model handled better (more power) and looked good.

However, driving with her less-dominant hand didn't allow for much sport-driving indulgence. Her left wrist throbbed its painful protest at being unable to steer the vehicle, so Naomi readjusted its position next to her (she needed to loosen the brace some). She drove her 540i above all, using the X5 for travel with over three passengers—as in, when in the car with both Leslie and Viv, or with Leslie and Leslie's mentor, Joy Giles, or when out on dates with Kevin, who preferred driving the X5 whenever they went out.

That last, she didn't have to worry about. She wasn't going out with Kevin; not now...or soon.

She listened to J.C. Bach's Symphony No. 1 in G major, Op. 6, letting the violins lift her spirits, deflating with thoughts of her situation (or lack thereof) with Kevin. The ride to her destination was uneventful but took forever when she finally approached and turned onto Bard O' Avon Court.

Interestingly, strains of the Supremes' "Someday We'll Be Together" drifted through the door as she rang the bell. The music stopped. Seconds later, the front door opened, and Naomi couldn't help smiling ear-to-ear. ...

BB: Pause Button

- What happens to Cecily's mental state?

- How will the Oscar-Naomi clash play out? FYI, the misuse of words/phrases in Oscar's chapter is intentional (you'll see).

- Where does Joshua fit in with all this?

- What happened with Kevin? Why is Naomi so excited? And how will this round of therapy go, given the other major issues at play (besides the home invasion PTSD)?

It's only the tip of the iceberg, Dear Reader!

Answers to these questions (plus other sexy, intense, and drama-filled events occurring throughout the story) await you inside both digital and bound formats at book retailers online!

Get *Broken Benevolence:*

I'll see you after "The End."
Until then, enjoy the story.

Thank you for previewing my series. The Dr. Naomi Alexander books have more in store, so I hope you're intrigued, ready to become a fan.

Learn more and indulge your readership with my stories and characters at sfpowell.com (and on social media with my Facebook page: author.sfpowell).

So, who's sitting on Naomi's couch next ...?

Book 4: Naomi provides therapy to four sisters...
Check online for info on pre-orders and/or availability!

Author's Postscript

My series features a fictional mental health professional, but mental health issues are real for many. If your mental health suffers, it also affects other aspects of your well-being. Overcome the stigma. If you or a loved one needs individual or family counseling, call 1-800-662-HELP (4357).

Well, Dear Reader:
Did you enjoy these previews? Intrigued? Ready to get involved with these characters and see how Naomi helps them?

Help Authors Telling Good Stories! Reviews Make a Difference.
Word-of-mouth can make all the difference for authors trying to attract readers. If you enjoyed a book in the series, please leave a review.

After "The End" ...
Naomi's counsel couch has a rotating cast of characters needing treatment, but what enlightening character details aren't the books revealing? There's plenty more to learn about the cast of the DNA, and it's reserved for fans of the series. Sign-up to get your booklover groove on with beyond-the-book DNA series content!

Also, connect with me via social media: like and follow my Facebook page (author.sfpowell).

About the Author

DC native S.F. Powell writes fiction focusing on life, relationships, and love in all its many forms.

Despite her full-time gig in accounting, she pursues writing, preferring rooms filled with book lovers over rooms full of ledgers and calculators.

Her stories touch on the elements of several genres because life is sometimes a suspenseful mystery carrying moments of romance and humor; maybe with enough drama, it seems right out of science fiction.

Her submission for *Like Sweet Buttermilk* (featuring fictional psychiatrist Dr. Naomi Alexander) won first place in the Black Expressions Fiction Writing Contest.

When she isn't absorbed with the written word, she enjoys game nights and generous goofy moments with her family, watching a documentary, or working on a puzzle.

Powell continues writing works featuring Dr. Naomi Alexander.

More information is available at sfpowell.com, or connect via social media (author.sfpowell).